GATHERING STORM

Center Point Large Print

**This Large Print Book carries the
Seal of Approval of N.A.V.H.**

GATHERING STORM

A Western Duo

LAURAN PAINE

CENTER POINT PUBLISHING
THORNDIKE, MAINE

This Center Point Large Print edition
is published in the year 2008 by arrangement with
Golden West Literary Agency.

Copyright © 2003 by Mona Paine.

The text of this Large Print edition is unabridged. In other
aspects, this book may vary from the original edition.
Printed in the United States of America.
Set in 16-point Times New Roman type.

ISBN: 978-1-60285-287-7

Library of Congress Cataloging-in-Publication Data

Paine, Lauran.
  [Calexico Kid]
    Gathering storm : a western duo / Lauran Paine.--Center Point large print ed.
    p. cm.
    ISBN: 978-1-60285-287-7 (lib. bdg. : alk. paper)
    1. Western stories. 2. Large type books. I. Paine, Lauran. Gathering storm. II. Title.

PS3566.A34G35 2008
813'.54--dc22

2008018123

Table of Contents

The Calexico Kid

Chapter One

What made it difficult for posse riders and at least one town marshal to catch the Calexico Kid was that there was nothing outstanding about him. In a territory where ninety-nine out of a hundred residents had black hair and dark eyes, were neither tall nor short, where outlaws were usually flamboyant to some degree, carried ivory-stocked six-guns or had silver on their outfits, the Calexico Kid rode a well-worn and use-darkened saddle, carried an old six-gun from which the bluing had been completely worn off, and some who had been his victims said he spoke English with no accent, others said he *had* an accent. Then there were those like the spinster-lady who had been on a coach he had stopped and robbed who said he spoke excellent English, was young and gallant, quite handsome, and was not very dark. She told the town marshal of Nogales that the Calexico Kid could be a Mexican, but because he was not swarthy, she thought he probably was a *gachupín*.

One early spring day he robbed the mercantile at Patagonia northeast of Nogales, locked everyone in a back room, and was gone before townsmen knew what had happened. The description was of a dark man neither tall nor short, nondescript in appearance, clearly experienced at his trade, things which, except for the spinster lady's romanticized wishful-thinking, fit the description of the outlaw known as the Calexico Kid.

At Tumacacori, Tubac, and Sasabe on the U.S.–Mexico border he had robbed stores and way stations in the early morning when shopkeepers were opening up, or later in the day when they were closing up. He was noted for appearing out of nowhere, speaking only to give orders, never raising his voice, being in all ways professional, and afterwards mingling with crowds or simply disappearing.

It helped that he had become a legend in a part of the country where heroes and myths were as common as tortillas, *fajitas, carne con chili*, and *entomatados*. Lawmen from Tucson to Sierra Vista, from Bisbee to Douglas, had hunted the Calexico Kid on the desert and in the mountains, in the villages, and even down across the line into Mexico. Lawmen were met with silence, shrugs, and blank expressions. He was to them the equivalent of the *gringo* Robin Hood. Their existence was hard, their lives a struggle from birth to death. They needed heroes, and, if the Calexico Kid was one of them, they held him in their hearts and enjoyed the times when he made fools of the *gringos*.

One summer day he stopped a stage midway between Tucson to the north and San Xavier Mission to the south, robbed the passengers, and took four sacks of U.S. Mail—and that, people would say much later, was his worst mistake. Robbing the mail was a federal offense.

He did not rob again until the following spring when he ambushed a party of sightseeing foreigners, four of whom were English. He robbed everyone down to the *gringos arrieros* in charge of the mule train, and departed on his bay horse. A fool among the visitors grabbed one of the weapons the Calexico Kid had confiscated and flung away, and fired at the back of the loping bandit, who twisted in the saddle without drawing rein and fired back. He hit the stranger squarely in the middle of the chest, and so something else was added to the legend of the Calexico Kid: he was one of the finest marksmen in the entire Southwest.

It was somewhat later, still early in the year but edging toward summer, when Deputy U.S. Marshal Dent Foster from Denver arrived in the Southwestern desert, the result of that mail robbery. He was a pale-eyed, graying, taciturn veteran of twelve years in federal law enforcement, altogether ordinary. In his earlier years he had worked in the Southwest. Most recently he had been involved in the cattle and sheep wars in the Montana-Wyoming country. He had been selected for his present assignment because he knew the Southwestern desert and spoke passable Spanish. He had been provided with names of lawmen to contact, but, when he arrived in Nogales, he settled in at the hotel, ate at both the local *gringo*-town café and the *cantina* over in Mex-town, contacted none of the lawmen whose names he had been given, and in his own unhurried, amiable way settled in.

Because his habit was to retire early and arise the same way, he was one of the first customers of the *gringo*-town café whose proprietor was one of those fleshy individuals who sweated when no one else did, was pale in a country where few others were, and used his apron to wipe sweat off his chin. He said: "Well, the son-of-a-bitch done it again, only this time he didn't kill no one."

Dent Foster raised a mildly interested glance. "Who?" he asked.

"That damned Mexican outlaw, the Calexico Kid." The fleshy man leaned against his pie table opposite Marshal Foster and crossed large arms over his chest. One of his three other diners paid up, grunted, and left.

One of the remaining diners said: "It's about time folks done somethin'. I been haulin' freight down here for five years, always worryin' about that damned renegade poppin' out of the brush. What's the point in havin' the law if no one makes it work?"

This diner also paid up and departed, only this time the departing diner stamped out of the café angry. The remaining diner, an older man, nearly bald with a half-moon scar down the left side of his face, leaned back, discreetly belched, and arose with twinkling eyes. He counted out silver, placed it beside his plate, and headed for the door as he said: "Nobody's asked me, but, if they did, I'd make a guess this Calexico Kid gets blamed for every crime that happens. It's got so that no matter what happens, someone steals a horse, robs a chicken house, run off with someone's woman . . . the Calexico Kid done it."

The café man waited until the roadway door closed, then grumbled: "Danged old screw-up, he never agrees with anybody."

Dent Foster gazed at the fleshy man, decided the café man was one of those people who, once convinced, would die before they'd admit they could be wrong, paid up, and also left the café.

Up at the saloon he finally heard the details. The barman was a sharp-featured, lantern-jawed person with the characteristics of a natural minder of other folks' business and gossip. He leaned on the bar as though imparting a confidence when he said: "You heard about the latest raid?"

Dent Foster shook his head.

"It was the Calexico Kid again. This time he got the money box off the southbound evenin' stage yestiddy."

Foster said: "Where?"

He was answered in a lowered voice accompanied by a conspiratorial wink. "Between here 'n' Patagonia, right smack dab in Dave Wheaton's back yard, so to speak." The saloon man straightened up. "Now let's see what that danged blowhard can do."

Dent Foster did not know whether the town marshal was a blowhard or not. He'd seen him around town but hadn't met him.

He went down to the livery barn, hired a horse, and

11

rode north out of town with a brilliant sun over his shoulder. The distance between Nogales and Patagonia was about a day's ride, but he didn't have to go that far before he saw a dozing horse tethered to a spindly tree, with the town marshal sitting nearby smoking, with his hat tipped down against the bounce back of sunshine off the roadway.

The larger and younger man arose, dusted his seat, ground out his smoke, and waited until Dent Foster had dismounted to say: "Are you passin' along or did you hear about the stage hold-up?"

Dent smiled, introduced himself. "Heard about it." He looked around. They were mostly in open country. He studied the berm on the far side of the road and said: "No tracks, Mister Wheaton?"

He got a short answer. "Sure. Help yourself," Wheaton gestured. "They go west from here plain as the nose on your face, past that field of brown boulders."

Dent Foster went into the shade. "He's long gone, Mister Wheaton?"

"It happened yesterday evenin'. There wasn't no sense to me comin' out here in the dark, and now it's close to midday. By now he's fifty miles from here an' still goin'."

Dent Foster was sympathetic. "A man can only do his best. Against this feller it'll take more." Foster squatted. "The trouble with hold-ups is that the outlaw has the first advantage. He shows up, robs, an' rides off. Lawmen don't even see his dust."

The younger lawman man came over to squat in shade, too. He gazed dispassionately at the older, graying man as he spoke. "This particular son-of-a-bitch knows the land, somehow he knows stage routes an' schedules, an', bein' a Mex', they'd hide him if the law came close. He's their hero."

"Who is?" Dent Foster asked mildly.

"The Calexico Kid."

"How d'you know it was him?"

Dave Wheaton scowled. The stage had been carrying a money box for the general store in Nogales, owned and operated by a slightly overbearing man of wealth named Ira Scott. "How do I know? Mister Foster, he's the only outlaw who raids hereabouts. An' the folks who've seen him know who he is. He's famous down here, the son-of-a-bitch."

Foster sat, squinty-eyed and silent, for as long as was required for him to begin to form an opinion. As he arose to ride back, he asked a question. "Do you have any idea how much money he's robbed off stages?"

Wheaton also stood up. "How much? Mister Foster, he's been robbin' stores, travelers, not just stages, for years. I couldn't even begin to guess how much he's taken."

"Is there a reward out on him?"

Wheaton nodded. "Three thousand dollars." As they untied their horses, snugged up cinches preparatory to riding back to town together, Dave Wheaton added: "He's more ghost than man. I've tried to track him a dozen times. He knows all the tricks, like dragging a blanket behind his horse, and I'd bet a year's pay the local Mexicans help him."

"How?"

"By hidin' him when he needs it, by makin' sure he always has a good horse under him, by actin' like they never heard of him when I talk to them."

By the time they reached Nogales, it was crowding suppertime. Dent Foster left the town marshal at the livery barn, hiked over to Aguilar's *cantina*, had a jolt of *pulque*, and ordered in Spanish, which interested the other customers, all of Mexican descent, all quiet in the presence of the only *gringo*. Foster ignored them. When his meal arrived, Aguilar lingered, watched Foster eat, and asked in Spanish if the meal was satisfactory. Foster raised twinkling eyes and said in Spanish: "I am eating it, am I not?"

The Mexicans laughed, even Pedro Aguilar.

Foster went to bed early and arose the following morning the same way. When he arrived at the *cantina*, Aguilar had just unlocked his front door. He welcomed Foster with an offer of *aguardiente* that Foster declined. It was poor quality liquor at best and belly-scalding before breakfast. He ordered eggs and coffee, waited until Aguilar returned with the platter, then invited him to share a glass of wine with him, which Aguilar did, since it was too early for customers and he was partial to red wine in the morning which was known to be a tonic. The fathers at San Xavier Mission strongly advised a glass of red wine before breakfast—it must therefore of a certainty be an indulgence sanctified by Him.

They discussed the stage robbery. Customers came and went. Aguilar had to leave to care for his trade, but, once the flow of customers slowed, he said: "There is no reason for it not to happen. Stages come and go." He shrugged heavy shoulders. "It is the only way passengers and money boxes arrive." Aguilar became very serious. "Why, can you tell me, don't those merchants who send money use armed out-riders? I'll tell you why, *compañero*, because they are too stingy. Especially *Señor* Scott. He is so stingy that when he finishes a cigar he grinds it into pipe tobacco."

Foster finished breakfast, pushed the platter away, settled back, and regarded his friend. "The Calexico Kid must be a rich man."

"Why?"

"Because he has been robbing for a long time. Years, I have been told."

Pedro Aguilar shrugged about that, excused himself to care for patrons, and only returned as Foster was arising to depart. Aguilar smiled. "He may be a rich man. The truth is I never thought about it."

Foster smiled back as he was turning away. "It costs money for information," he said, walking out into bright sunlight and leaving Pedro Aguilar standing like a statue looking in the direction of the doorway.

Later in the day Foster met the town marshal at the saddle and harness shop. Foster lingered after the town marshal had departed and the saddle maker, an old, vinegary individual, threw a contemptuous glance in the direction of his doorway. "When he first come here, he'd ride 'em down until hell froze over an' for two days on the ice." The old man spat amber at a nearby spittoon that sat in the center of a low, wooden box full of sand. He missed the spittoon but hit the sand, shifted his cud to the other cheek, and considered Foster, who was no longer young, either. Older men had a kind of affinity. He said: "Years back he'd make up a posse and never let up until they was found . . . then they'd get hung." Warming to his subject, the saddle maker wiped both hands on an old stained apron, leaned on the counter, looking at Foster, and scowled. "Y'know what's wrong with this country, pardner? Book law. There's fee lawyers nowadays. Our way was better. Catch 'em an' hang 'em to the nearest tree."

Dent Foster agreed, and the saddle maker got them both a cup of coffee from his little iron stove, asked where Foster was from, which was as near to a personal question as etiquette allowed.

The coffee was too hot. Foster eased the cup away and also got comfortable against the counter. "Montana, Wyoming, other places." He did not allow the saddle maker to ask another question. He asked one of his own. "Who the hell is this Calexico Kid I been hearin' about?"

The vinegary, thin, wiry man answered gruffly. "A

Mex' bandit. He's been raidin' the countryside for five, six years."

"From what I've heard, he makes a good livin' at it. That coach he stopped north of town had a money box on it. If he stops enough of them, he should be able to retire."

The saddle maker watched traffic pass out front. "They never quit, mister. You're old enough to know that. They most likely figure they're bulletproof." The old man straightened up, gazing at a moist hide on his cutting table. If it dried out too much, he'd have to sponge it again. As he placed a tin *rosadero* pattern on it with his back to Foster, he said: "Ride 'em down. Keep goin' until you catch 'em. Settin' on your behind in town never caught one an' never will."

Foster went over to the mercantile where an over-weight, balding man with pale skin and a massive gold watch chain across his middle was behind a counter. They exchanged nods. Foster bought a sack of Durham tobacco, and, since the only customer in the store was in the dry goods section being cared for by a young man wearing black sleeve protectors from wrist to elbow, Dent leaned on the counter: "I'm a stranger to Nogales. Looks like I come at a bad time." He began a smoke as he spoke. "Where did he get that name . . . Calexico Kid?"

The hefty man said: "That son-of-a-bitch. That's the second time this year he's got away with money I've sent north to a bank."

Foster lighted up looking mildly surprised. "The second time?"

"Yes. An' I'll tell you somethin' else, mister. If our town marshal'd do somethin' besides shakin' his head and wringin' his hands, he could track him down."

The merchant's indignation did not deter Foster. He asked again where the Calexico Kid had got that name. This time the storekeeper acted annoyed. "How the hell would I know? I'm goin' to write the U.S. marshal up in Denver. Maybe the Army, too."

Dent Foster was sympathetic. "Offer a reward. Maybe that'd help."

The storekeeper scowled. "There's already three thousand dollars out on him. Did you ever hear of such a thing? Three thousand dollars! Why, hell, they didn't have that much out on the James brothers. For that much money I could point out fifteen men in Nogales who'd turn in their own fathers."

"No results?"

The storekeeper swore. "No! Not a gawd-damned whisper."

Later, Foster visited the corral yard of the stage company and talked to a dark, thick Mexican named Epifanio Gonzalez who had a pock-scarred face, and still later, about suppertime, he squatted in the dust behind the hotel. Using a little stick, he drew lines where stages had been stopped, and smoked a cigarette while studying the stick tracks. Eventually he arose, scuffed out the stick map, killed his smoke, and went around front to enjoy the pleasant evening from a chair on the verandah.

He watched the town close down for the night a little at a time, was roused from his reverie by the arrival of a southbound stage accompanied by four heavily armed, capable-looking outriders. It turned in down at the corral yard, was in there for less than half an hour, emerged with a fresh hitch, and drove south without even stopping for the outriders to get fed.

Two men emerged from the corral yard to stand together in the failing light of day, staring after the coach as it cleared the southern end of town and vanished from sight. One of those men Foster recognized by his build—the yard man, Epifanio Gonzalez. The other one he could not identify. He was as tall as Gonzalez but trimmer. He made a guess he was the stage company proprietor.

Dent Foster spent the ensuing two days on horseback. He visited the places where stages had been stopped, sat on low top outs studying the countryside, and passed arroyos where a mounted man would be invisible from the upper, flatter country. He talked to people in distant *jacales* scraping out an existence, asked no questions just visited, then rode on. By the time he was ready to settle on the hotel verandah again, he had a fair knowledge of the entire area, almost all the sites where the Calexico Kid had struck, and where he might have gone afterwards. On this subject, he was clear about one thing—the natives he had talked with had shown closed-down faces and had said only enough to pass the time until the *gringo* rode on.

Chapter Two

One early summer evening Foster and Pedro Aguilar sat in the *cantina* enjoying red wine and talking. Foster told stories of his experiences years earlier as a range man. He mentioned his life on the Southwestern desert. Aguilar kept their glasses full and told of his experiences, some humorous, some not. He had lived hard until his fortieth year. After that he had settled in Nogales' Mex-town, opened his *cantina*, and was now content to grow heavy and, by his own admission, lazy.

They made a compatible pair; neither talked too much, and both had humor. Both were past the age of great ambition and quick tempers. Aguilar knew Epifanio Gonzalez, the yard man for the stage company. He rolled his eyes about their acquaintanceship. "He isn't even very good-tempered when he is sober, but when he drinks . . . Chihuahua! He rode with *pronunciados* . . . he was a *bandolero* who raided along the Texas border. He was a hired *pistolero* to protect Madera."

"He told you all this?" Foster asked, and sipped red wine.

Aguilar shrugged. "He is single . . . most of the time,

anyway . . . so he eats at my *cantina*. I've known him for maybe four, five years." Another shrug. "You know how it is . . . men share a few drinks . . . they talk." Aguilar chased a blue-tailed fly from his face with a large hand. "I'm surprised he's lasted so long with Carter Alvarado. You know Carter?"

Foster shook his head as he emptied the glass.

"He owns the stage company. I thought everyone knew him."

Foster arose and reset his hat. "I've only been here about a week," he said, nodded, and walked back toward *gringo*-town.

There was a raid on a *gringo* horse herd west of Nogales between Sahuarito and Tubac in an area where few people lived. It was worthless, semi-desert as far as a man could see. In springtime there was grass. By midsummer it was gone. It had been the custom of *gringo* stockmen from as far northeast as Benson to drive livestock to the Southwestern desert for the graze until midsummer, then drive them elsewhere after the grass was gone.

Town Marshal Wheaton took three townsmen with him and was gone four days. He might as well have remained in town. The raiders had come in the night, had made their gather, and had run for the border. The *gringo* cowman and his riders had gone after them. When the tracks crossed the line down into Mexico, they had turned back. By the time Marshal Wheaton met them it was too late. Even if they had wanted to continue the pursuit into Mexico, there was an excellent reason why they didn't. One of those Mexican revolutionary armies was camped at the border smack dab where the tracks went.

There was no question concerning the identities of the raiders, nor was there any doubt about who got the horses. Mexican revolutionary armies were always in need of saddle stock.

On the day after Marshal Wheaton left town, a stage was stopped north of Nogales near Tubac. It had been carrying passengers from as far west as Bisbee. It had skirted inland as far as Sierra Vista, then had dead-headed directly cross country on a slightly downward curve to Nogales, where it had discharged passengers, picked up other passengers and some light freight, acquired a fresh hitch, and had gone north without incident until a man on a bay horse had appeared in the roadway with a cocked six-gun.

Mr. Scott at the Nogales general store had a fit, not only because he had lost another money box, this one going north to Tucson, but also because Marshal Wheaton was off somewhere supposedly chasing horse thieves. Scott went before the town council, hammered a tabletop with his fist, got beet-red in the face, and gave the town council an ultimatum—either they fired Dave Wheaton and hired a better man as town marshal, or he would import as many gunmen as he could find and take over law enforcement himself.

The councilmen were more apprehensive than intimidated. The storekeeper had one of the most lucrative businesses in Nogales. He had the kind of money that was required to hire gunmen, and after his explosion at the council meeting not one of the councilmen doubted he would do exactly as he had threatened to do.

Foster heard about the robbery and rode north to the place where it had occurred. He was not surprised when he arrived at the same site where he had met the town marshal a week or so earlier, all open country except for that boulder field a hundred yards westerly. Same site, same highwayman, same technique. He poked around for tracks and found an endless assortment of them on the roadbed, but no tracks elsewhere as there had been before, and no tracks going west.

He rode back to Nogales, turned in his hired horse, went up to the hotel to sit in overhang shade, relax, and have a smoke. Later, close to suppertime, he went down to Mex-town. Aguilar's *cantina* was empty except for an old man dozing in a corner of the room. He was very dark with white hair and a big, fierce, white mustache. Aguilar set up two glasses of *cerveza*, would not take money, and said: "I make it myself. The first drink out of every batch I try out on customers. Drink . . . tell me what you think."

Foster drank, put the glass down, ran a sleeve across his lips, and nodded with considerable gravity. "Very good. As good as I've drunk in a long time, and, Pedro, I never was much of a whiskey man. I like beer, and this is very good."

Aguilar beamed, tasted the beer himself, and agreed

with Foster. "It *is* good. . . . Well, you went riding after the robbery, eh?"

Foster's pale eyes considered his friend. "*Huarache* telegraph?"

Aguilar laughed. "People see things." He shrugged, then leaned down on the counter, considering Foster closely. "We talked once about the Calexico Kid. You said by now he must be a rich man. You remember?"

Foster nodded, drained his glass, and went to work on a cigarette. As he lighted up and trickled smoke, the barman spoke again. "*En el pais de las ciego, el tuerto es rey.* You understand, *amigo?*"

Foster understood. "Yeah. In the land of the blind the one-eyed man is king."

"Well, you asked about the Calexico Kid. Today you went up where a stage was robbed."

"By the Calexico Kid?" Foster asked quietly.

Aguilar reverted to Spanish. "Who knows? But you think so, no?"

Foster slowly inclined his head as he trickled smoke. Their eyes were fixed on each other.

Aguilar then said: "I'll tell you what I think, companion. There is for you an interest in the Calexico Kid."

Foster smiled and used English. "Pedro, you're *coyote.*"

"I am the one-eyed . . . the others are blind. Are you interested in him?"

Foster punched out the smoke in a dented tin can, one of many along the bar for smokers. He hung fire over an answer, but eventually smiled when he said: "I'm interested. So is Mister Wheaton, an' right now so is the man who owns the general store. So are a lot of people."

Aguilar straightened up off the bar and sighed. "Another beer?"

Foster nodded, watched the dark, heavy man go to draw off two more beers, and waited until Aguilar had returned before saying: "You didn't like my answer?"

Aguilar put a strained look on Foster. "Do I look like a fool? It wasn't an answer. It was an evasion."

Foster hoisted the second beer in a slight salute that Aguilar returned, just barely. After they had half drained the glasses, Foster asked a question: "Are you interested in three thousand dollars?"

Pedro Aguilar leaned down on the bar top again, his eyes fixed and inscrutable. "Is that how much bounty they have put on him?"

"Yes. And the storekeeper'll likely add to it. Why does he make a point of robbing the storekeeper's money boxes?"

Aguilar's shoulders moved slightly. "Because he is the only one who has a lot of wealth."

Foster finally had his answer. *Because he has a lot of wealth* was the same as saying to Dent Foster that the Calexico Kid knew about the storekeeper's financial affairs, when he would receive or send money. And *that* pretty well settled for Dent Foster, not the identity of the Calexico Kid, but why his most lucrative raids were made in the country north of Nogales.

After supper he returned to the hotel verandah, shoved out his legs, got comfortable, and watched the lights and shadows along the street. He saw Dave Wheaton emerge from the jailhouse, pause, then head for the saloon. He also saw the portly storekeeper who wore that gold chain across his paunch lock his building for the night and turn southward.

The man from the corral yard emerged from his office that fronted on the main thoroughfare, locked up after himself, and strolled north. Foster watched the man. He was slightly more than average height, had dark hair and eyes, pleasant, even features. Foster decided he was handsome.

The man stepped onto the hotel porch, nodded to Foster, and disappeared past the front door. Foster continued to sit for about fifteen minutes, then arose, and ambled down to the corral yard where two carriage lamps showed the wide gateway, one on each side. There was a thick, tall pole set into the ground midway into the yard. Atop it was a lighted lantern that, because the mantle was clean, cast considerable light around the yard.

Foster stood outside, watching two men, one the burly, pock-marked man, taking their time rigging out a four-horse hitch that was already partially harnessed to a faded, durable-looking stagecoach. Gonzalez growled a couple of times at his helper; otherwise, both men worked in silence. Along the far back wall there was a bunkhouse built into the northwest corner. Intentionally or not, whoever had built it hadn't had to fabricate two walls, the westerly and northerly ones. Otherwise, there were stalls, all empty, and farther back a pole corral. There were two gates, one facing the yard, another one in back of the corral leading out into an alley.

Foster strolled southward, crossed down through a dogtrot between two buildings, emerged in the alley, and walked northward as far as that alley gate from the holding corral. From there, he followed the alley until it crossed a side road west of the hotel, then continued on northward to the upper end of town where there was open country. He lingered up there, admiring the night, the stars, the air as fresh and clean as though it had rained recently, which it hadn't, and most likely would not do so again until next winter.

He returned to the hotel, bedded down, slept the sleep of the just, awakened the following morning, and after a visit out back to the wash house went down to the café for breakfast.

The man next to him at the crowded counter wore black cotton sleeve protectors from wrist to elbow. Foster spoke to him while waiting for his meal. "I'd guess your boss was mad about that coach being robbed north of town."

The store clerk turned. "Mad? Mister, he could have chewed bullets an' spit rust. That's the third time since last winter."

Foster's platter arrived. He ate for a while, then spoke to the store clerk again. "Mister Wheaton will maybe find him."

27

The clerk snorted. "Dave Wheaton couldn't find his backside using both hands. Mister Scott's thinkin' about hirin' some outsiders."

Foster nodded about that. "Gun hands?"

"Yes. Mister Wheaton," said the store clerk, biting off each word, "can suck eggs. I been in Nogales seven years, an' I'm here to tell you, as far as I know, he never even caught no chicken thieves. It's a mystery to me why the town council keeps him on."

Chapter Three

Later, Foster strolled as far as the saddle and harness shop, was greeted with a bird-like nod by the vinegary proprietor who was rolling cuts of leather into damp sacks. The old man wiped his hands on his apron and asked if Foster would care for java. Dent agreed, and, as on his other visit, the coffee was too hot and smelled more like brimstone than coffee. He nursed the cup without raising it as the cranky, sinewy older man said: "Well, what'd you think of that? The Calexico Kid stopped another coach, robbed it, and sent it on its way . . . and Dave Wheaton warn't even in town." The old man drank scalding coffee as though his gullet was pure rawhide, and scowled fiercely at Foster. "Y'know what I think, mister? I'd like to know for a fact where Dave was when that stage got stopped." The fierce look lingered. The saddle maker narrowed his eyes a tad. "It wouldn't be the first time, would it?"

Foster agreed that it wouldn't be the first time a lawman broke the law. He changed the subject. "That feller who owns the stage company . . . he must have got descriptions from his drivers."

The old man grunted. "Sure. There's descriptions from hell to breakfast. He rides a bay horse, nothin' outstandin' except that he does his work professional-like an' sends the coaches on their way."

"I meant what he looks like," Foster said, easing the cup farther along the counter.

"Mexican, dark hide, black hair and eyes. Like I said, nothin' outstandin'." The old man faced Foster across the counter near his cutting table, eyes bright and fierce. "If Dave Wheaton had the guts God give a goose, he'd go down into Mex-town and rattle some cages. Them folks stick together closer'n peas in a pod. Mister, they laugh every time the Kid makes a raid. Not at him, at us, at *gringos*."

Foster asked the question he had been leading up to. "How would folks know the feller who raided the coach day before yesterday up north was the Calexico Kid?"

This time the old man returned to the counter to lean before addressing Foster the way he might have spoken to a child, and maybe a not very bright one at that.

"I come into this country thirty-two years ago, back when folks wasn't sure whether Nogales was in the United States or Mexico. Back then it was all a man could do to keep from getting bushwhacked by Mexican border jumpers from below the line, an' danged

29

Indians. Not until about four, five years ago was there anyone called the Calexico Kid. Startin' back then is when he commenced raidin'. I got no idea who fixed that name on him, nor why they done it, but take my word for it, up until four, five years ago there wasn't no Calexico Kid raidin' in the Nogales country." The old man paused for breath before continuing. "This is his territory, an' until we get rid of Dave Wheaton, get a real lawman, the son-of-a-bitch will go right on raidin'."

"How about killin'?"

"Well . . . some time back he shot a feller who was packin' for some foreigners squarely in the chest, but to me anyway that don't fit my idea about him. Hell, if he'd been a killer, he would have killed before this. Don't it seem likely?"

Foster agreed that it did seem likely, then went over to the saloon to sit in a dark corner with a glass of beer.

Whether it was Marshal Wheaton's fault or not, there was no denying that he had failed badly with the Calexico Kid. Maybe, as the saddle maker had intimated, the Kid was too smart for Dave Wheaton. If that was so, then he must also be too smart for a lot of other folks, the difference being that it was Wheaton's job to catch the outlaw, and other folks, like Scott, the storekeeper, with a lot of anger but no experience wouldn't know how to go about catching any outlaw, let alone an experienced, *coyote* one like the Calexico Kid.

Foster babied his beer, ignored the noise over at the bar, decided he had two particular things to do to settle his suspicion, went over to the hotel, and bedded down.

In the morning he went over into Mex-town for breakfast. By now he was recognized and nodded to by Pedro Aguilar's customers.

Aguilar served Foster at one of the small tables and lingered until Foster looked up enquiringly. Aguilar said: "I went to bed last night thinkin' about you. I'll tell you straight out . . . you look less like a lawman than any I've ever seen."

Foster continued to gaze at Aguilar without speaking.

The heavy, dark man said: "But you are, aren't you?"

Foster nodded toward a chair. "Sit down."

Aguilar couldn't. He had customers. He said— "Wait."—and walked away.

Foster waited. If patience was a particular virtue, Dent Foster possessed plenty of it. He waited through the last of Aguilar's breakfast trade.

Aguilar's apron was soiled, his shirt hadn't been washed in days, and, as he sat down at the little table with a bottle of red wine, he smiled as though ready to laugh uproariously over a private joke. He had from lifelong habit recognized lawmen on sight. This time he had been made a fool of, which was very funny to him.

He poured two glasses half full of wine, raised his glass in a salute, and drank. He afterwards blew out a breath. His dark eyes twinkled with irony. "You don't look the part," he said. "Lawmen're big, mean-lookin', younger. . . ." Aguilar shrugged. He regarded Foster with that bemused, ironic expression for a silent moment. Being a product of his time and place, Pedro Aguilar had principles that he did not allow to interfere with personal feelings. He liked the gray, unassuming man opposite him. He said: "Well, *compañero*, three thousand dollars is a lot of money."

Dent Foster quietly nodded.

"But . . . at my age, satisfied finally that I'll never be a rich man, and being contented now, tell me . . . what would I do with three thousand dollars?"

Dent Foster made no attempt to reply. He sipped wine, relaxed, and waited. Intuition told him Aguilar did not expect an answer.

Aguilar emptied his glass. "First, let me tell you . . . a man can't live here as long as I have without seeing and hearing things. You called it the *huarache* tele-graph. That was very good."

Foster wondered how long this was going to take and rolled a smoke. He raised his eyes when Aguilar said: "Did you know a stage passed through last night with armed outriders?"

Foster nodded and trickled smoke.

"He missed that one." Another shrug. "Just as well. It was carrying an Army payroll south and west to a soldier encampment near Sierra Vista. Because there is a revolution going on down in Mexico, the U.S. Army has been moving in."

Foster narrowed his eyes to avoid smoke as he thought that *huarache* telegraph was maybe even better than the other kind.

"He couldn't have stopped it . . . not against four armed guards. But if he could have, he'd never have had to rob another stage. You understand?"

Foster punched out his smoke as he nodded, raised his gaze to Aguilar, and softly said: "Who is *he?*"

Aguilar's ironic twinkle returned. "You know who. The Calexico Kid."

Dent Foster emptied his glass, and Pedro Aguilar leaned to half fill it. As he did this, he said: "We're friends. Friends ask questions and deserve honest answers, no?"

"Yes."

"You are a lawman?"

"Yes."

"What kind . . . a sheriff?"

"No. A deputy United States marshal."

Aguilar's brows shot up. "Here, where there is nothing but hardship and desert?"

"He robbed a stage carrying U.S. Mail. That's a federal crime."

"I see. He made a mistake, eh?"

Foster nodded.

"Well . . . you know Epifanio Gonzalez?"

"The stage company's yard man? Yes, but only to nod to," Foster replied, and faintly frowned. "Not him, Pete."

Aguilar smiled. "No . . . listen to me, *compañero* . . .

I wouldn't sleep well if I told you any more. You understand?"

Dent Foster understood. A resident of Mex-town who had a *gringo* friend had to draw the line somewhere. He could be helpful for the sake of friendship, but he could not do more.

Foster returned to *gringo*-town, went up to the saloon which was opposite the corral yard, got a glass of beer, and sat back in shadows where he could clearly see past the stockaded gates into the corral yard. He saw several men working over there. Twice he saw the company's owner, Carter Alvarado, come into the yard from his office and talk with Epifanio Gonzalez.

Later, Foster went in search of the telegraph office, found it in the heart of Nogales, in the midst of a cluster of stores, sent a message to Denver, and returned to the hotel to loaf and watch the corral yard, consider each vehicle that came and went, not just stages but also light wagons and once a high-sided, old, battered freight rig being pulled by six Mexican mules, smaller than Missouri mules, but just as hardy, tough, and durable.

One afternoon Foster and the town marshal played a game of checkers at the *gringo*-town saloon. Wheaton was not in a good mood. "That 'possum-bellied screw-up who owns the mercantile wants the town council to fire me," he told Foster, while jumping one of Foster's red checkers.

"Because of the raid south of town while you was lookin' for horse thieves?"

"Yeah. That, an' Mister Scott ain't hardly spoken to me for a year. I told the council what you said . . . outlaws got all the advantage, 'specially if they raid just ahead of sunset which gives 'em all night to leave the territory."

Dent Foster leaned to concentrate. He was blocked in every direction, so he had to sacrifice one red checker, and, while that move gave him one of Wheaton's black checkers, the town marshal struck back by taking three of Foster's red checkers.

He smiled for the first time since the game had started. Foster smiled back. The town marshal needed something to change his mood, and, in fact, when they had sat down to play, Dent Foster had no intention of winning.

Foster considered his diminishing corps of red checkers as he said: "Wheaton, the Calexico Kid's raidin' ground is pretty much local territory."

The town marshal's reply was short. "No. He's raided dang' near up as far as Tucson."

"Where do you suppose he hides out?" Foster asked, and got another abstruse, illogical reply.

"Anywhere. He's a Mex'. They'd hide him, an', hell, Foster, it's a big country down here. I've tried to track him. I've rode my butt raw. They're hidin' him sure as hell, but findin' anythin' out from them people is like pullin' teeth. All they do is give a man a dumb look and shrug. But I'll find the son-of-a-bitch if it's the last thing I ever do. He's around . . . somewhere. I'll find him. In fact, tomorrow mornin' I'm goin' to ride down a story one of the stage drivers heard about someone raisin' smoke in a big arroyo northwest of town, which is where outlaws have hid over the years . . . I'll get him, for a damned fact."

Dent Foster ate early and sat on the hotel verandah watching traffic diminish as dusk arrived. The following day he met the stage company's yard man at the saloon in the mid-afternoon.

Gonzalez gave Foster one of his curt, unsmiling nods of recognition and said: "You got a job yet?"

Foster turned his beer glass in its wet pool as he replied. "No. It seems folks in town don't hire often, an' for the last few years, when I try to hire on as a rider, they look at my gray hair an' hire younger fellers."

Gonzalez's response came from a man soured on life. "They always got some reason, don't they? I should have stayed in Mexico. Down there I never had no trouble findin' work. Up here, you got to take whatever scraps they want to toss your way."

Foster leaned and nodded, fitting his mood to that of the yard man. "You know what I think? They'd spit on you, if they dared."

Gonzalez turned slowly and regarded his companion. "That's a fact. What's your name?"

"Dent Foster." As the burly yard man extended a

36

hand, Foster smiled. "It never mattered before when we met . . . what's yours?"

"Gonzalez. My name is Epifanio."

Foster smiled again, signaled the barman for two refills, and got comfortable against the bar again. "This one's on me," he told the yard man

When their drinks arrived, Gonzalez said: *"Gracias."*

"No hay de que."

Gonzalez looked at Foster. *"¿Habla español?"*

Foster shrugged. *"Un poco."*

They spent an hour drinking and talking. Other patrons came and went. The barman, always curious, always nosy, hovered. When he did that, they would switch to Spanish, and, when he moved away, they would grin and exchange a wink. It was a pleasant time. As with Pedro Aguilar, Dent Foster was in no hurry. Even when he asked about the man Gonzalez worked for, it seemed to enter their conversation naturally.

Gonzalez's response was totally unsuspecting. "He's a good man to work for. In fact, I've been with him longer than anyone since I came north. You met him?"

"No, but I know him by sight."

"His mother was Mexican, his father a *gringo*. He was born somewhere in Colorado. He come here an' started his stage company five, six years ago."

"It is successful?"

Gonzalez gazed into his empty glass when he

replied. "*Sí*. Very successful. Last night one of them bullion coaches passed through. It had outriders. Even the gun guard and driver were closed-mouth, mean-actin'."

"Where was it going?"

"To the Army over near Sierra Vista," Gonzalez replied.

Foster studied the pock-marked man's face. Gonzalez looked gloomy, disappointed, Foster thought. Shortly afterwards he paid up, slapped Gonzalez on the shoulder, and went up to the hotel to bed down.

The following day he rented a horse, rode down to the telegraph office, got his message from Denver, and rode back to leave the horse and go over to Mex-town. It was late afternoon. Pedro Aguilar had only recently seen his last tequila customers head home for supper. He leaned on the bar, watching Foster cross from the old spindle doors showing no expression except up around the eyes. When Foster asked for *cerveza*, Aguilar did as he'd done before: he brought two glasses. He said: "How is the manhunt going?"

Foster tasted the beer. It was warm the way beer should be, and it had a pleasant, yeasty aroma. "I bought Gonzalez drinks the other night. You were right about that payroll stage." Foster paused, looking steadily at Aguilar. "He wasn't happy to see it go."

Aguilar made an exaggerated sweep of the bar top with a moist rag from beneath the bar. It gave him time to frame his next question.

"Are you a careful man, *amigo?*"

Foster nodded. "Always."

Aguilar smiled slightly. "You had better be."

By the time Foster left the *cantina*, the day was ending. He emerged from a dogtrot in time to see Gonzalez and Carter Alvarado part in the middle of the corral yard after what had evidently been a long palaver.

He went to the café, ate, hiked up to the saloon, and encountered Marshal Wheaton up there. The town marshal had been drinking, perhaps on an empty stomach, because, when Dent Foster walked in, he turned from the bar and spoke loudly of their checker game and how easy it had been to beat the graying, nondescript-appearing man crossing toward the bar.

No one laughed and the saloon had a fair crowd. The sharp-featured saloon man brought Foster his beer, and this time Marshal Wheaton went too far. His face was sweat-shiny, his eyes were unnaturally bright, and, when he sneered at Dent Foster and spoke loudly again, the barman froze behind the counter, just below which he had an ash spoke on a shelf.

"Too old!" Wheaton loudly exclaimed, clearly for the benefit of the customers. "When a man gets your age, Foster, he'd ought to go back to playin' mumblety-peg."

Foster half emptied his beer glass, and pushed it away. After Pedro Aguilar's *cerveza* this beer tasted like vat dregs.

Dave Wheaton was stung at being ignored. He

shoved back from the bar facing southward, down where Dent Foster was leaning. "Foster, you want to play mumblety-peg?"

Dent turned slowly, quiet, calm, and expressionless. The barman spoke to the town marshal. "Dave, leave it be, you're drunk."

Wheaton whirled on the barman. "No one gets drunk offen that diluted coal oil you serve for whiskey."

Foster saw the barman's right shoulder drop as he felt for the ash spoke. He addressed Wheaton as the barman stood perfectly still.

"Marshal, get some fresh air."

The town marshal faced around and glared. "Foster, you been askin' a lot of questions around town, an' I don't like snoopy people."

Dent Foster gently shook his head. "Go home an' sleep it off, Marshal."

Popskull impaired co-ordination. When Dave Wheaton started his draw, Dent Foster seemed barely to move. His six-gun barrel was aimed slightly upwards, in the chest area of Dave Wheaton, as he said: "One of you gents take his gun." When no one moved, Foster cocked his six-gun. "Drop it, Wheaton. Go home an' sleep it off."

Wheaton was standing like a statue when the ash spoke hit the back of his head. He collapsed without a sound. Foster holstered his sidearm, gazing at the man on the floor. The barman asked two townsmen to carry their town marshal down to the jailhouse and dump him there. As two volunteers moved to comply, the barman spoke to Dent Foster.

"I'll apologize for the damned fool. The town council raked him over the coals this afternoon. I've never seen him get drunk so fast before." The barman rapped the counter with the ash spoke and raised his voice. "Drinks on the house, gents."

Dent Foster went up to the hotel, more annoyed than angry. His last thought before dropping off to sleep was that maybe Scott and others were right, maybe Dave Wheaton ought to go back to range riding, or whatever he had done before becoming town marshal. One thing was an undeniable fact. He didn't have the brains for the job, and, after what had happened over at the saloon, as far as Foster knew, he didn't have good judgment, either.

Without his knowledge of it, his face-down of the town marshal and his deadly fast draw became topics of conversation—and speculation—the following day. People he had barely noticed nodded and smiled when he went down for his breakfast.

His presence in the café had a noticeable dampening effect on conversation. The fleshy café man brought his meal in record time and refilled his coffee cup twice before it was even half empty.

Chapter Four

By afternoon there was a rumor that he had been hired by Mr. Scott of the mercantile to do as Mr. Scott had threatened to do: to bring law and order to Nogales. By evening every man in Nogales who was over fifty was feeling twenty years younger. An older man had vindicated their private opinion that older men were just as good, and maybe even better, than younger men. Foster noticed the change, the deference, and was annoyed by it. He had been shying clear of notoriety most of his life, and right at this time he had other, more pressing things on his mind.

The following day he made up a bundle, wrapped it in strong brown paper, secured it with sealing wax, left it in his room, and went down to the mercantile to ask Mr. Scott if he could leave the package in Scott's safe until Foster could make arrangements to have it sent north to a savings company in Tucson.

The storekeeper raised his eyebrows. "Is it money, Mister Foster?"

"Yes. I've got no idea when the next northbound stage leaves. I'd take it kindly if you'd keep it in your iron box until. . . ."

"Mister Foster!" exclaimed the large, pink-skinned, paunchy man. "You know about the raid a couple days back on one of Alvarado's stages? Don't ship your money north on one of his coaches. I've been raided three times already this year."

As the merchant's face reddened, but before the big vein in the side of his neck throbbed, Dent Foster made a puzzled frown and asked a question. "Seems to me, if I'd lost money off three stages the same year, bein' carried by the same company, I never would've sent the second and third boxes."

Ira Scott considered Foster as though trying to decide whether he was being criticized or what. He lowered his voice. The clerk in sleeve protectors was not too distant. He was checking the contents of shelves and writing on a clipboard seemingly not the least interested in what his employer and Dent Foster were discussing.

"The second an' third times the funds from the store weren't sent in regular money boxes."

Foster gazed steadily at the fleshy, large man. "You had it hid?"

"Yes, sir. The second time in a bolt of gingham cloth. The third time at the very bottom of a keg of horseshoes."

Scott reared back staring at Dent Foster, who had not heard this story, but had assumed, as evidently everyone else around town had also assumed, the merchant's losses had been locked inside regular money boxes.

Dent rolled a smoke, and lighted it. The clerk was still taking inventory, only now he was moving farther toward the gloomy back of the store. His employer lighted a fragrant cigar and shook his head at Dent Foster. "You got the bundle with you?" he asked. Dent shook his head. He said it was hidden at the hotel, that he'd get it and bring it back.

Outside, he stamped his smoke to death, went as far as the bench in front of the store north of the café, and sat down. He slouched there, wondering if Scott was as dense as the town marshal. He was killing time.

Later, he returned to the general store where the clerk met him. Ira Scott was down at the café having a late dinner. Foster asked the clerk to tell Scott, because it was very urgent that his money bundle get up to Tucson, that Foster had decided to take a chance on the afternoon northbound from Nogales.

He went up to the corral yard, met the proprietor, Carter Alvarado, asked when the midday northbound coach would leave, told Alvarado he had a package he wanted delivered up in Tucson, and was assured it could be done, even though the stage scheduled to leave directly would be slightly delayed. Alvarado stood in the middle of his corral yard, watching Dent Foster cross to the saloon.

Foster had plenty of time for a drink. The stage wouldn't be ready to go north for another hour. He got his glass of beer, took it to the poker table in the shadowy back of the room, cocked back his chair, and sipped beer as he watched the corral yard.

For a supposedly smart merchant, Scott had been clever, concealing his money as he had, but what Dent had been told about Scott's being stingy had as sure as God made green apples assured the money would be found and stolen, where, if he hadn't been as tight as the bark on a tree, he could have hired armed out-riders, common practice every place Dent Foster had ever been when valuables were involved.

Dent Foster sat a long time gazing across the sun-bright roadway. When he saw a coach being wheeled into the center of the yard, he left the saloon, went up to the hotel, got his sealed parcel, took it down to the corral yard, handed it to Carter Alvarado, was assured for the second time the package would be delivered to Tucson, hiked briskly down to the livery barn, hired a long-legged grulla gelding, rode up the alley north-ward, past the palisaded alley wall of the corral yard, and left town at a loose gallop. He held to that gait until, sitting twisted, he could distantly see a banner of dun dust a short mile north of town.

He rode into a tumble of tan boulders, dismounted, settled in for the long wait he expected, and saw a rider loping upcountry west of town, as though he hadn't turned north until he was about a mile to the west. Now he was paralleling the stage road and moving fast. Dent smiled to himself. Because it was the custom to walk a hitch of horses about a mile to warm them out, the oncoming horseman, who had increased his speed, passed the coach with more than a mile separating them. If there were passengers on the stage, they might notice a distant rider on their left, but with no reason to be concerned they wouldn't pay undue attention.

Dent lifted out his six-gun, made a cursory, reassuring examination, and returned the weapon to its holster.

The stage was managing to stay ahead of its dust, but just barely, evidently the whip favoring his horses for the long haul, which was wise because, although the full burden of summer heat hadn't begun to bear down yet, it would bear down before this day was over.

Mistakes and errors are a part of life. In fact, they at times appear to be a *daily* part of it. Mostly they were correctable, which was not the case when determined armed men were involved. Foster had been concentrating on the rider and the coach. He missed seeing a second man, this one sitting a horse north of Foster's boulder field, partially obscured by a stand of dainty paloverdes and the patchwork shadows they projected. He was sitting as motionless as a statue watching the stage, the oncoming rider, and Dent Foster's back.

When the stage hauled back from a trot to a walk, Dent lifted his hat, mopped sweat, re-set the hat, and twisted to see where the rider was. He was still a fair distance southward and he, too, had slackened pace but not down to a walk; he was riding at a steady lope. He would reach Dent before the stage did, and that was a cause for worry. Dent knew enough about the rider to know he would not be easily ambushed.

He hadn't really expected events to be orderly. In his line of work they rarely were. By taking his grulla where boulders were horse-high before returning to the lower rocks where he had a sweeping view of the roadway, well within six-gun range, he wanted to know more about the oncoming horseman. The horseman was no more than a mile, maybe a mile and a half, from the boulder field, which was probably his destination since there was no other cover except those paloverdes that Foster had dismissed with one glance as an ambushing site. He had done it not only because were they poor cover; they were also beyond accurate six-gun range.

The coach was at least two miles southward under a yellow sun and summertime's faded blue sky. It was no longer scuffing much dust as the hitch plodded along with loose lines.

The heat was increasing, which Foster ignored. Shortly now the stage would be close enough. He lifted out his six-gun at about the same time the shade silhouette among the paloverdes swung to the ground and unshipped a booted saddle gun.

The oncoming horseman was distinctly recognizable—Epifanio Gonzalez, sweating as he headed for the boulder field, the site Foster was convinced the Calexico Kid had struck from during his earlier raids.

It was an ideal ambushing site, close enough to the road with huge boulders for concealment. Foster had been convinced of that some time back when he and Marshal Wheaton had hunkered ten hours after a hold-up, and Wheaton had said the tracks went due west. At that time Wheaton had been too demoralized to follow the tracks. Any other lawman, demoralized or not, would have followed the tracks, would have found where the highwayman had been waiting.

Foster shook his head. Wheaton had told Dent that the Calexico Kid knew how to blanket-out his sign, and, as far as the town marshal was concerned, that was the end of it.

Foster's speculation was cut short as the yard hostler stopped and looked southward, probably estimating the distance where the stage was still making steady, slow progress behind its walking hitch and himself. He talked to his horse. Foster knew about where Gonzalez would enter the boulder field because there were only two or three openings wide enough to accommodate a mounted man.

What happened next Foster should have anticipated. The grulla horse nickered. Instantly Gonzalez halted. His mount was standing head high, peering in the direction from which the call had come.

Dent Foster wiped sweat from his palm down one trouser leg and scarcely breathed. Gonzalez was close to being beyond accurate six-gun range, and he had a carbine slung under his right *rosadero*.

Behind Foster, the shadowy silhouette among the paloverdes knelt to watch. He leaned on his Winchester. Because Foster was among the boulders and hadn't faced toward the paloverdes, the kneeling man had no idea who he was.

The coach was readily distinguishable in every detail as it came up the road still at a walk. Foster had no time to look around or speculate. Gonzalez had dismounted and, using his mount as a shield, stood on the animal's far side as he rested the Winchester across the saddle seat.

All Dent Foster could see was legs and a head behind the saddle gun. He hadn't expected Gonzalez not to be very experienced.

The yard man called out, first in Spanish, then in English. "Who is it? Stand where I can see you."

Foster did not move from his crouch between two boulders. He heard Gonzalez lever up a cartridge into the Winchester's firing chamber. Even with a Winchester there would have been little for Foster to aim at unless he shot through the horse.

The stage was close, barely three hundred yards to the south, when the man among the paloverdes fired. Foster was showered with rock splinters. Completely surprised, instinct made Foster drop flat before trying to look back.

Gonzalez, also startled, raised his head squinting toward the paloverdes.

A voice Foster recognized called out. "He's in the rocks on your side."

Gonzalez, also, recognized that voice. The stage was almost parallel with the boulder field when the whip yanked back on his lines, as startled as Foster had been. Inside the coach a woman screamed. Also inside a man's bull-bass yell told the whip to turn back, turn the damned coach around.

Gonzalez recovered fast. The man in the rocks was

not who he was supposed to be, but the voice from among the paloverdes was as familiar to the yard man as his own voice.

Gonzalez fired once across the saddle seat. His horse jumped and sprang wildly. Gonzalez held one rein in his left hand. He was exposed when the frightened animal reacted to the muzzle blast.

Foster raised up, carefully aimed, and fired. The burly yard man went down in an awkward fall, lost the rein, and his horse fled, head and tail up, in the direction of Nogales. The stage driver was fighting his hitch, trying to turn back. Gunshots terrified horses. It was all he could do to keep the stage from tipping over as the horses made a turn too abruptly. The coach came up off the ground on the near side. When the frightened horses lunged, the coach was slammed back down.

Foster heard the whip profanely encouraging his hitch in its wild escape. He was watching Gonzalez whose leg had been broken above the knee. The yard man was writhing and threshing. He no longer held his carbine.

Foster belly-crawled until his back was to Gonzalez. The man among the paloverdes was invisible; only his horse was discernible. Foster ground-sluiced twice. His second shot must have struck something close. The horse spun and raced out into the open. It, too, made a beeline for town.

The invisible gunman was belly-down where shadows made it almost impossible to make him out.

Only when he returned Foster's fire did the federal officer locate him, but all he could fire at was the muzzle blast. The man himself was still invisible.

Once more the man among the paloverdes fired. He had better range. It may have occurred to him that the ambusher in the rocks did not have a Winchester, only a six-gun, but if it did, it was too late.

Foster had been waiting for that second shot. He took a long rest over his left forearm, squeezed slightly, and was nearly deafened when his Colt roared and bucked backwards.

The man among the fragile little trees half rose up, flopped onto his side, scuffed briefly, and became still.

The sun was slightly off center. It's force was at its peak. Foster did not move. He reloaded and waited. Someone from town would be along when that coach got back. He was soaked with sweat.

Gonzalez was making groaning noises. He was still writhing on the ground.

Foster considered Gonzalez as a mild peril. It was the man among the paloverdes he was concerned about, but, after firing three times into the little trees and receiving no gunfire back, he began slowly and warily to arise from among the rocks. He could barely make the man out, but where his Winchester had fallen was a good thirty feet from where the man was discernible. Unlike Epifanio Gonzalez, the other man was not moving.

Foster took a chance. With his back to the writhing yard man, he went up to the paloverdes, picked up the

Winchester, and stood a long time gazing at the man who had used the saddle gun. One of Foster's slugs had struck inches below the hairline. The man was stone dead.

Chapter Five

Later, he went down to where Gonzalez's face was sweat-shiny and twisted from pain. He brought the dead man's Winchester with him.

Foster tied off the bleeding, flung Gonzalez's guns as far as he could, then went back to the grulla horse, rode out of the rocks and down the road toward Nogales.

He had ridden about two miles when he encountered riders, nine of them, all but one Nogales townsmen. The one who was not gazed at Foster after the others had gone northward to find one wounded man and one dead man. He said: "Dent, I got to Nogales this morning. No one knew where you was. The liveryman said you'd hired a horse." The speaker was a stocky, sun-bronzed individual with a perpetual squint. "Then that stagecoach come into town with passengers scairt peeless an' the driver yellin' at the top of his lungs. I joined the posse comin' up here."

They turned back toward Nogales. The stranger had a canteen. Foster drank a third of its contents and fresh sweat burst out all over him. He eyed the other man as he said: "You got the message from Denver?"

"Yeah. I was over near Tombstone an' rode myself raw gettin' down here. Are you all right?"

"Yeah, I'm all right. Jess, I'm gettin' too old for this. One of 'em was behind me. That's never happened before. An' I let my horse nicker."

The other deputy U.S. marshal turned his squint southward. There were others who said Dent Foster was too old and ought to retire, but Jess Brigham and Dent Foster had been friends for years. Jess did not like the way their conversation was going so he changed the subject.

"What happened back there? Them folks on the stage was almost hysterical. They yelled and run around like a herd of chickens. Any dead ones back there?"

"One. Did you ever hear of the Calexico Kid?"

"Yeah. He's back there?"

"Dead. He's the one I didn't know was behind me. There's another one, a yard man for the Kid named Gonzalez. I figured most of it out, but from what I heard the Calexico Kid rode alone. He didn't. He had Gonzalez ride separately. To back him up if there was trouble, I expect. I watched the wrong man, Jess. I watched Gonzalez."

Foster had another long pull on Brigham's canteen. They rode the rest of the way in silence.

The day was wearing along. When they had town in sight, shadows were thickening. There were a few lights. There would be more in another couple of hours.

They tied up out front of the mercantile. Jess followed Foster inside where Ira Scott was tallying his daily receipts and his young clerk with the black sleeve protectors was clearing a nearby counter. Like everyone else in town they had heard what had happened. They stopped what they were doing and stared at Foster and the stocky, unsmiling man with him. Foster ignored the clerk to ask Scott a question: "Did you tell anyone at the corral yard you hid that money in the bolt goods an' the horseshoe keg?"

Scott shook his head without speaking.

"Who helped you put the money in the package of cloth and the keg?"

"Me 'n' Andy put it in there. Andy's my clerk."

Foster faced the man with the sleeve protectors. "How much did Alvarado pay you?"

The clerk was white to the hairline. He spoke in an unsteady voice. "Pay me for what? I don't know what you're talkin'. . . ."

Foster drew his six-gun and cocked it. "How much did Alvarado pay to tell him where the money was cached? Lie to me an' I'll blow your head off. *How much?*"

"Fifty dollars."

Foster holstered his gun as he said: "Mister Scott, take the son-of-a-bitch over to the jailhouse. Tell Marshal Wheaton to lock him up."

Scott didn't move. "Wheaton quit this morning an' left town."

"Take him over there an' lock him up yourself."

The large man stared briefly, then jerked his head at his clerk.

Outside, people on both sides of the road stopped to gawk. Foster jerked his head. "Let's go get somethin' to eat. No, not down there, over in Mex-town."

Pedro Aguilar had already heard. In fact, he knew something Dent Foster didn't know. Epifanio Gonzalez had been brought back to town by the town's posse men. He had been brought back upright. Carter Alvarado had come back, too, tied belly down across the seat of the saddle of the man riding his horse from behind the cantle to prevent the corpse from falling off.

Aguilar told them to take a table, went to his cooking area, and worked fast. He had several customers, but the atmosphere in the *cantina* had become unpleasant. They finished their meals swiftly and departed. They, too, had heard what had happened.

Foster and his friend were eating when three men arrived from *gringo*-town, the saloon man, the saddle maker, and Ira Scott. Others would have come, but Scott scowled them out of it.

Aguilar offered them chairs. The saddle maker and the saloon man accepted, but Scott remained standing. "He's locked up," Scott told Foster, who nodded without looking up. "An' he told me about it."

Foster stopped eating and looked up. "Did he tell you who Alvarado was?"

Scott and his companions looked blank. "He told me he give Alvarado the information about when I was sendin' money north and how I hid it." The merchant's brows dropped. "He worked for me seven years. I paid him well, treated him good. . . ."

Dent Foster continued to regard the storekeeper. Maybe he had paid the clerk well. Maybe he had also treated him well. If there was one thing twelve years as a lawman had taught both Dent Foster and the man across the table from him, it was that dishonesty didn't seem to require a reason.

The saddle maker growled at Scott. "Ask him."

The storekeeper cleared his throat. "Mister Foster, with Dave Wheaton gone there's a vacancy, an' the town council'd like to offer you the job."

Foster didn't reply. He fished in a shirt pocket, palmed his federal marshal's badge, shook his head, and went back to his meal.

The townsmen lingered briefly, clearly surprised to know that the graying, nondescript man they had come to know was a deputy U.S. marshal.

After they left, Pedro Aguilar appeared with his jug. The three of them drank red wine. Aguilar refilled their glasses, and, while his eyes were watching as he poured, he said: "Gonzalez is at the midwife's house." He finished pouring, and set the jug aside as he raised his eyes to Foster.

"You killed a local hero, Marshal."

Foster, in the act of raising his glass, stopped moving. "You knew who he was?"

Aguilar shrugged.

"Others knew, too?"

Again the shrug.

Foster continued raising his glass. He looked straight across the table at Pedro Aguilar as he said: "To the hero . . . the Calexico Kid."

All three men downed their wine. After the pair of federal lawmen left, Aguilar leaned for a long time on the counter before a dark old man with a fierce, snow-white mustache shuffled in, ignored Aguilar, went to a chair, sat down, and closed his eyes.

Aguilar watched the old man, then swabbed his bar top as he softly said: "I knew it. It was those mail sacks. He was a fool to take them. What good are a lot of letters. If a man dies, it should be for something great and heroic . . . not mail sacks."

It was dark before Dent Foster and Jess Brigham found the midwife's house. It was small and old. The woman herself was the same, small and old, but also broad and dark. She took them to the dingy room where Epifanio Gonzalez was lying. His face was sweaty and flushed. His eyes were bright. Beside the bed there was a rickety table with a glass and a jug of red wine on it.

He eyed Foster and ignored the other federal lawman. "So it was you. We became friends." Gonzalez made a death's head smile. "Who told you?"

"The store clerk."

"Ah? That bastard. I told Carter. . . ."

"It wouldn't have saved you or Carter." Foster again palmed his little badge, and this time Gonzalez reached for the glass, half emptied it, and shook his head. "The sacks of mail. I told him it was crazy. He said people sent money in letters. A ton of mail sacks wouldn't make us as much money as stages made us."

Foster was leaning in the doorway. "Gonzales, where did he get that name . . . the Calexico Kid?"

"He started robbing along the California-Mexico border. That's what they called him over there. It got too dangerous. He came here. He started robbing stages, mostly his own. I hired on with him when I left Mexico ahead of the *rurales*." Gonzalez reached for the glass, which was empty, so he shoved it irritably aside. "Well, *amigo*," he said sarcastically. "What happens to me now?"

Foster eyed the filthy, bloody bandage on the outlaw's leg as he said: "I've got no idea. *Vaya con Dios,* Epifanio."

The night was dark with a puny moon when they returned to the roadway. Jess Brigham mentioned what Dent Foster had been thinking back there.

"The old woman is a *curandera*."

Foster nodded. "Yeah. She's letting him drink himself unconscious. We were lucky. We talked to him before he got dead drunk." Dent looked at Jess Brigham. "How long does it take blood poisoning to kill a man?"

"Maybe a week, maybe ten days."

Brigham was wrong. Epifanio Gonzalez was dead within three days. The final irony for Gonzalez was that, when the Mexicans to whom the Calexico Kid was a hero, created the song of his exploits, his heroism, to perpetuate his myth, they did not include Epifanio Gonzalez in any of the stanzas of their *canciones*.

Gathering Storm

Chapter One
TWO KINDS OF MEN

Buckrum's livery barn had a long, wide alley that was usually well raked and wetted. It made the interior of the old structure at least ten degrees cooler inside than it was outside, where the gouging sunlight leached the sweat out of men before it got fairly out of their pores.

Ed Smith watched Rezin Hartman count out adobe dollars—four of them—and his eyes behind the thick glasses were eager. He took the money and jerked his head to shake off a blue-tailed fly that had left the circling coterie of his fellows and landed on his neck. Rezin looked up.

"What stall'll you have him in?"

Smith had anticipated the question. Hartman's two guns, tied down and black butted, had given him the clue. "He'll be in the fifth stall down, on the north side."

Hartman nodded, looked around as another rider loomed up in the wide doorway, looked back at the big grulla horse he had dismounted, and snapped another question at Smith, who had beckoned to someone down the gloomy, cool lane. "Tack'll be all right here?"

"Yes, sir." Smith nodded curtly. "There's always a man here. Days and nights." He looked past Rezin, saw the newcomer standing beside his horse, hipshot and silent, black eyes in a swarthy face raking over the barn hawkishly, and smiled at Hartman. "Night man'll have the keys to the tack room, and I'm here during the day."

Rezin nodded, turned on his heel, and walked out. He stabbed a quick glance at the dark stranger. Their eyes crossed electrically. Each nodded a tight, brusque acknowledgment and looked away. Ed Smith walked over to the dark man, pocketing Hartman's adobe dollars.

"Yes, sir?"

"How much to keep him?" The flat-brimmed, low-crowned hat jerked toward the horse.

Ed looked him over. He was a big black. Leggy, deep-chested, and breedy-looking. Ed knew horses and men. He could've told what kind of a horse Rezin Hartman, and this other man, would have ridden, if he'd never seen the critters. Fast, durable, breedy animals.

"Dollar a day inside and grained. Outside, in the public corral. . . ."

"Inside and grained." The mahogany hand held out the reins. Ed took them. "Too much, though."

Smith said nothing.

The black eyes swept over the interior of the barn again. "Where'll he be kept?"

Ed knew the man would ask that. Like Hartman had. He nodded, taking two silver cartwheels from the stranger. "Fourth box stall down on the north side."

"Who was the *hombre* rid in just ahead of me?" The hat slanted toward the grulla. "Man that rode that horse?"

Ed shrugged. "Don't know him. Stranger. Probably a cowboy. Spring roundups're going full blast in the Brazitos. Lots of travelers now. Cowboys and transients coming and going every day. Used to be. . . ."

"Yeah. Yeah." The stranger cut him off, turned abruptly on his heels, and stalked toward the street.

Ed watched him go without another word. He saw the tight, muscular litheness of the man and the two guns lashed to his legs with their yellowish, ivory handles. He sighed and faced away as an old man with sour body odors drifted up, his watery blue eyes bleary and moist. He handed both horses to the hostler with a sigh.

"Two of them, Cleat. Two of them the same day. You might say the same hour and minute . . . almost."

Cleat looked myopically toward the gaping doorway, where the raging sun made him look away. "Two what? Drummers?"

"Gunmen, Cleat. Bad sign when two of them come to Buckrum the same day. Same minute, almost. Bad sign."

Cleat looked at the horses. "Yeah. Well . . . what d'you want me to do with these?"

"Put the grulla"—Smith squinted at Hartman's horse—"looks like a ridgling to me . . . put him in the fifth down on the north side. The black goes in number four, north side. Mind you don't get them mixed up, Cleat." Smith looked at the rifle butts jutting upward out of saddle boots. "They're all the same. Soon's they hand you the reins, they want to know what stalls they'll be in. Always grained, too. Any time you want to know whether a rider'll ask you that question, look and see if he's wearing two guns. Gunmen always want to know where their horses'll be stalled. Never fails."

Cleat turned away disinterestedly. "Yeah, grulla in five, black in four. North side."

Rezin Hartman would have beaten the other rider to Buckrum by an hour except that he had by-passed the town to ride down a grass-choked old wagon trail, remote and vague with neglect, that led him to an abandoned ranch. Its sightless windows, like empty eye sockets, looked out over the shimmering land from a sturdily built house with a squatty log barn a hundred feet or so from the shattered picket fence with the lost gate.

He had sat his horse, looking in at the ghostly old place for a full ten minutes before he had ridden back over the summer dry CL range to Buckrum. The visit had stirred distant memories within him. The pained look was still in his eyes, as when he had left his horse at the livery barn. That's why Rezin Hartman arrived at Smith's barn only a moment before Owl Russel did.

Owl walked about fifty feet from Smith's barn and leaned against the front wall of the Buckrum Land and Abstract Company's shoddy little building, under the warped overhang. He methodically rolled a cigarette, although he rarely smoked, and swept the sun-blasted little cow town from under the brim of his hat. He was a lean, hard man with a mighty chest and shoulders, where stringy, round muscles had been punched solidly inside the mahogany-colored skin.

Buckrum was like a hundred other villages in the raw new empire that he had known. Manure scattered liberally over the dusty, rock-hard roadway that ran north and south, and a clutch of buildings leaning on each other wearily for support against the wild elements that wore them down, warped their rough boards, and blistered their cheap paint. He studied the Parker House Hotel and Saloon with more than passing interest. It was directly across from where he loitered. Up the road, on his side of the plank walk, was another little bleached building with a handmade sign that said: OFFICE—SHERIFF OF BRAZITOS COUNTY. Owl Russel looked beyond that, contemptuously, to the scattered houses, some swathed in faded tar paper, all without paint, and then brought his glance back to the Parker House Hotel and Saloon. He smoked lazily, indifferently, watching the people go by. The men were all either cowmen or freighters. The women— what few were abroad in the killing heat—were bonneted and frocked from instep to neck, like so many ambulatory statues. Owl's eyes went over each one hopefully, then gave up.

He thought about the man who had arrived in the livery barn just ahead of him, and his two guns. He had noticed something else, too. Something the livery man hadn't noticed. There had been a glint of anguish in Rezin Hartman's eyes. Standing there idly, getting the feel and lay of Buckrum, Owl Russel speculated on the other two-gun man's presence.

Rezin was inside the Parker House Saloon, at the upper end of the bar, where it swung up against the wall, while Owl Russel was making his instinctive appraisal of the town. He ordered an ale and paid for it with another adobe dollar. The brew was tepid, but it was wet and tangy, like acrid oil, and cut the scorch and phlegm in his dry throat. He finished the first and nodded for another. The bartender, a man known only as Frosty, fished his pay out of the change left from the first drink, and ignored the stranger with the bronze-gold hair showing below the gracefully upcurving edges of his Stetson.

Conseil Purdy's jet-black eyes were pinpointed on the fair-haired two-gun man from his tiny table over close to the office door. Purdy owned the Parker House Hotel and Saloon, and, except for the top being gone off his right ear—lost in a long-forgotten knife fight—he was nondescript-looking. His eyes were watching Rezin Hartman with acute interest. His heart was beating a little faster, too. Purdy had almost made up his mind to get up and go over to Hartman when the louvered doors swung inward and Owl Russel walked in. Surprise, then perplexity, chased each other over Purdy's dark features. He frowned and absently chewed the inside lining of his cheek. Here were two gunmen. He'd sent word down the back trail for one. Now which one was his man?

Owl Russel fixed the barman with his cold glance, and let the clock tick four times before he ordered. "Whiskey mash."

Purdy appraised the ivory gun butts swooping outward from the man's hips. He had little patience and wanted to know which of these killers was going to do a job for him. He watched as Owl Russel drank the mash and ordered another, blew out his chewed cheek, and sipped his ale. Damn coincidence, anyway!

Rezin admired the staid, substantial look of the old saloon, with its cool gloom and feeling of drowsiness. He noticed the customers were the usual run of cowmen, grizzled and hard and gray, with a sprinkling of cowboys on the town, younger, flashy, loud, and obviously at loose ends, as though charged with the fabulous discovery that they were free men—or, rather, free boys with men's bodies. He saw Conseil Purdy, too, pegged him as the saloon's owner by his bearing and dress, which included a huge gold nugget that sagged over his thick chest from a massive watch chain. He also recognized Owl Russel as the man he'd seen enter Smith's livery barn as he'd left that place. There was a seedy-looking eagle, poised in perpetual flight, its glassy eyes staring into eternity, high over the bar. A little of the stuffing showed through one parted seam. Furtively Rezin watched the swarthy gunman down whiskey and mash drinks like they were water. He marveled.

Owl Russel was on his third drink when he turned and saw Con Purdy sitting in the tiny booth near his office door. He stared with his usual wide-eyed look, until Purdy's eyes wavered. Owl noticed the notched right ear. Strangely there was something akin to recognition in the ebony eyes, recognition and startled, bitter humor. He took up the drink and walked over to Purdy's table, stood above the man staring down, saying nothing.

Purdy could feel the sweat in his armpits. He didn't even try a smile. "You like birds?" he asked.

Russel nodded, still staring boldly, half contemptuously, downward. "Yeah, owls."

Purdy relaxed a little and inclined his head toward the bench opposite him. Owl sat. "Five hundred for a dead Indian."

Owl rolled the whiskey around inside his mouth. Frosty made a good sour mash. "Where is he?"

"Shack about two miles from town, along the river. Got goats staked around the place. You can't miss it. Stick to the river. His name's. . . ."

"The devil with that. Got the five hundred?"

Purdy felt the chill at the table, like Owl Russel hated him, or at least as though the gunman held him in abhorrence. He shrugged uncomfortably. "Not here. In the office." He started to get up. "Come on."

Russel finished his drink. "I'll wait. Go get it." He watched Purdy walk to the office door with a thoughtful look. Then he shook his head ever so slightly, shrugged, got up, and went over to the bar, caught the barman's eye and flicked the empty glass at him with a brusque nod. The fourth drink came back to him promptly. He paid for it without taking his bold eyes off Frosty, turned abruptly, and went back over to Purdy's table, and sat down, his spurs making tiny music in the drowsy room.

Purdy handed over the money without a word. Owl stuffed it into a pocket, arose abruptly, as though something distasteful were there in the booth with him, and walked back over to the bar without a backward glance. He saw Hartman's blue eyes flicker over him, and ignored them. Rezin was too still and quiet to warrant Owl's attention.

Rezin had seen men drink ale like that before, but not hard liquor. Not whiskey mash. He finished his second ale, sighed, shoved off the bar, and walked across the saw-dusted barroom, out of the doors onto the duckboards just outside. A million flies arose frantically as he ducked around the hitch rail, with its animal burden, and crossed the dusty roadway, gathering furry edges of tan dirt on his boots and spurs. He stepped up onto the plank walk on the opposite side of the road, hesitated before a grimy, specked window in the Buckrum Land and Abstract Company's building. Inside, he could see a fat, sweating old man drowsing alone behind a desk. He went over and knuckled past the door.

Burt Hunt forced up his eyelids with an effort, let them drop for a delicious second of relapse, then shot them upwards, and started violently in his chair at sight of Rezin Hartman. The gunman's face was blank and watchful.

"Rezin! By God, boy. . . ."

"Never mind that, Burt. Where's Antrim?"

The older man's pale flesh with its oddly blue pouches under the weak eyes seemed to fade even more. A pained look jumped into his eyes, pained and insistent. "Listen, Rezin. There's been enough trouble over that. God, boy, it was twenty years ago. Leave it be, son. Listen, I've lived a long time. I know best. Never was a killing that didn't get another one. Two killings're bad enough. Don't make. . . ."

"Where's Antrim, Uncle Burt?"

Hunt's mouth closed gradually. An old clock ticked serenely, lazily, above a rack of pine filing cases. A fly caught in a spider's web buzzed excitedly. "Please, Rezin . . . son. Don't make it any worse. You're young. There's. . . ."

"You don't tell me, Burt, I'll find out anyway." Rezin stepped backwards to the door, let his fist rest on the cool knob, and looked down at the older man and noticed how little gray hair was left on his skull over the sweat-beaded, pale meat. "Where is he?"

Burt Hunt looked at the whipcord body and the smooth, deceptive strength of the younger man, and said nothing. A flurry of old memories jerked and jumped behind his eyes. He shook his head.

"Rezin. . . ."

Hartman twisted the knob savagely. "I'll find him,

Uncle Burt." The icy-blue eyes were thoughtful. "You're a coward, aren't you?"

Hunt heard the words over and over, long after the door had closed behind the two-gun man. They ricocheted off the dingy walls again and again. He let his head go forward into his hands and lowered both to the desk top. *You're a coward . . . you're a coward. . . .*

Rezin got his information accidentally, and significantly, when he was walking toward the livery barn. Two cowboys passed him. One chuckled and his words spilled out through his mirth. "Ol' Bull'll be sore as hell. He thinks I'm out checkin' the out range for CL strays, north of Salt Licks."

The other rider snorted derisively, edging off the plank walk into the roadway, steering for the Parker House. "Ah, the devil with Antrim. He's nothing but a foghorn, anyway. I'm supposed to be. . . ."

Rezin watched them go through the buggy traffic, weaving in and out. His memory filled in the missing pieces. He'd been only eight years old the last time he was on CL range, but he recalled the cottonwood-lined lane to the main ranch well. It had been a wonderful place for hanging imaginary rustlers, for a youngster. He continued on toward the livery barn, saw Owl Russel swing out through the wide doors on his big black horse, heading south. He avoided looking at the dark man and forgot about him as soon as he had saddled his own animal, swung up, and rode southwest across the great, scorched range where annoyed bunches of CL cattle brushed under willows and sage to rid themselves of the everlasting flies.

Rezin rode like an arrow, straight to the edge of the CL heartland, where the scored and sullen knob of Razorback Hill separated CL headquarters from the abandoned ranch he'd stopped at earlier. It didn't take long to tie the grulla three cottonwoods back from the entrance to the shimmering ranch yard. He skirted the glare-ridden yard proper, swung inward from the east, and walked, stiff-legged, into the yard itself, where he stopped, flexed himself automatically, and hollered.

"Antrim!"

Nothing happened. Rezin saw the sleepy, drowsy horses in the pole corral by the big log barn, and guessed the hands were taking a *siesta*. The sweat ran down under his shirt along his ribs and irritated him. He saw the ageless old ranch house with its sagging verandah and wilted climbing roses. A memory of Cliff Lewis, big and hard as rock, flitted across his vision.

"Antrim!"

The second yell was louder. He saw a patch of movement over at the owner's house. A large, stooping man came outside, rubbing sleep-swollen eyes. His gray hair was tousled and he was in his stocking feet. He squinted against the glare at the single man standing in the middle of the yard, weaving in the heat waves.

"Who you want?"

"Antrim."

"Oh. Holler again. He's in the bunkhouse." Cliff Lewis turned toward the screen door sluggishly. Rezin watched him with the pleasant knowledge that Lewis wouldn't recognize him anyway. Twenty years made a lot of difference in a young man. Not so much in older men.

A third voice growled into the sun-blasted silence: "Yeah? Who're you? What you want?"

Rezin saw him standing in the bunkhouse doorway, scratching his thick middle. "You, you murdering son-of-a . . . !"

Bang!

Antrim jumped violently, sagged, made a frantic pass at the slab doorjamb, and fell forward. Rezin saw him bring up his single gun, and waited. He knew the shot wouldn't be close. It wasn't. His right hand *clicked* again, rose slowly, froze, and vomited another slug. It was better that Antrim's gun showed one fired cartridge. Rezin's second bullet made Antrim's feet drum on the floor inside the bunkhouse, while his spatulate fingers made peculiar climbing gestures just over the edge of the bunkhouse stoop in the dust. His gun was lying beside him.

Rezin was running, sucking the blast furnace air into his lungs where it felt like hot tar. He didn't see old Cliff Lewis start violently at the shots and whirl away from the screen door. He never looked back until he was untying the grulla.

Then he shot a fast look as he slammed into the saddle, spun away, and careened down the lane in a flurry of speed. Inside the CL bunkhouse, five horri-fied cowboys were rooted to the floor. They heard the drumming of a shod horse racing over the land, and didn't move.

Owl Russel saw the tethered goats first, turned off among them, watching in the dead grass for the picket lines. The black horse was foot-shy. He'd go berserk if he got tangled in one of those stake ropes. Owl cursed the ropes, the beady-eyed goats that were regarding him with quick interest, the myriad flies that buzzed him, and the sun—the sun worst of all.

Owl rode low through the willows that ran back fifty feet or so from the sluggish slattern known as the Little Brazos River. The willows were shade, but they hadn't been cut overhead enough to allow a horseman to pass. He reined up at sight of a crude shack and called out.

"Injun!"

There was a casual flap of burlap hung for a summer door in the shack that faced the stinking river. A dark hand flipped it aside, and a tallish, blocky Indian stepped through. His hair was coarse and jet-black, but his face had the hair-crack lines of age on it. His features were open and curious as he came out. A look of shock and surprise was rising up when Owl's gun thundered and bucked backwards against his thumb pad. Owl's horse shied suddenly at the noise and swung the saddle off center. Russel cursed shortly, swung down, shoved the saddle back on center, and gave the latigo a little tug, still holding his gun and looking over at the hovel.

The noise had awakened a small boy. He came drowsily out of the shack, looked somberly at his dead father uncomprehendingly, turned, saw Owl Russel's big black horse, and his eyes kindled with admiration. He saw Owl, too, but the horse held his attention. He took several tentative steps forward, smiled brightly all over his fat, oval face, and ran quickly forward, hands out to pet the big horse. Owl holstered his gun, blinked at the child, stooped down, scooped up a handful of little pebbles, and tossed them. The little boy, not over five years old, came on undaunted. He brushed Owl's leg and reached out to touch the horse. Russel stood, left leg poised in the stirrup, the brilliant sunlight glinting off his silver overlaid spur, regarding the small boy. The little Indian patted the black's leg. Owl swung up, reined away, and spurred out of the willows. He caught sight of an Indian woman bearing two water buckets, coming from the direction of the river. She was hurrying through the reeds with a puzzled, apprehensive look on her face.

He rode back past the goats, watching for the stake ropes again, cleared the area, and blew his nose with his fingers to shed the offensive odors of the place. The sun burned into him like fire, but the flat-brimmed hat shielded the obsidian, black eyes. He turned northward and jogged over the range watching for sign of riders. The Brazitos country was somnolent, however, under the whiplash of blistering heat.

Siesta was a wise custom the new rulers of the land had gratefully adopted from the old rulers—the Mexicans and Indians. Owl rode alone through the writhing, shimmering daylight.

There was a crawling, insistent sensation under Owl Russel's skin before he found the freight road up north, swung onto it, and rode leisurely back toward Buckrum. He was approaching the town from the opposite direction of the Digger's shack. The inner discomfort made his features even more forbidding and brutal. The black eyes were masked, however, and calm enough, when he swung down at the livery barn and handed the reins to Ed Smith without a word. But the black eyes, trained to observe, noticed that Hartman's grulla wasn't in the stall. He wondered carelessly why Rezin had ridden out in the midday heat, then shrugged. Rezin Hartman meant nothing to Owl Russel—yet.

Owl Russel didn't mean anything to Rezin, then, either. Rezin waited for pursuit for half an hour, decided it must have by-passed him, since he had twisted northward as he had fled, mounted, and rode out of the willows where he had waited. The land was dead in the dazzling light. He let the grulla pick his way along in the general direction of town and cleaned his gun as he slouched along. The sweat was making irritating rivulets under his clothing. He ignored them, he thought—but older, wiser hands would've known that this same dripping, tickling, annoying heat was what made men's tempers short and knife-edged.

The sun was quite a bit overbalanced with the weight and conscience of the spent day by the time Rezin broke over onto the Buckrum road. For an inexplicable reason, the knowledge that he was heading back to town made him feel better than he'd felt in days. Far ahead he could dimly make out the shifting outlines of a double-tongued freight caravan pushing its sluggish way toward Buckrum. He wondered at the way the crazy sun made everything shimmer and dance, then forgot it in favor of a more satisfying thought.

Bull Antrim was dead. In effigy, back up in Wyoming, Rezin had planted the bullets there hundreds of times. The second slug—after he had cannily let Bull get in his single shot—had finished the job. That, too, was planned. Even the dryness in Rezin's throat didn't detract from the sense of exultation. There were more laws than the one that burdened itself with a nickel shield. There was the law of retribution—the law of revenge, the laws of books and written rules, the law of honor, and the dread law of vengeance! Bull Antrim had mysteriously evaded all but the last. On the frontier, *that* law was known as the most fitting and just of all laws. Rezin Hartman believed in it as did all the other rough men of his time. It, more than any written law, made men prudent and thoughtful in a lawless land.

The freighters swung out around Buckrum, as was

their custom, heading for the hereditary campground of their kind. Big billows of full-bodied dust rose lazily in the dead air as the mighty wheels turned in the dry earth. The sun was fast giving over its cowed domain of scorched soil to the late afternoon shadows.

Rezin rubbed his horse dry in an old buffalo wallow where salt grass grew, interspersed with ragweed. Then he re-saddled and rode on in. Ed Smith was gone for the day, but Cleat came out of the gloom and took the grulla from its rider and led it away. Rezin, on the spur of the moment, plunged his arms into the water trough just outside the barn and splashed the coolness over his face. Methodically, then, he dumped his Stetson on the back of his head and exhaled loudly. Bronze-gold hair tumbled damply over a broad forehead as he hiked over the duckboards toward the Parker House Saloon.

Listless men standing or sitting apathetically in the shade paid him slight attention. The heat seemed to leach the vitality from everything it touched—horses, men, even the ever-present urchins playing in the roadway, and their nondescript dogs. Rezin eased through the slatted doors on their greased spindles and felt the vital coolness, and smelled the time-honored mellowness of a saloon.

Frosty was busy with the pre-evening trade and brought Rezin's ale after a harassed delay. The saloon was half full of sweaty men: cattlemen, and teamsters from the freight camp on the outskirts. The rank odor of old sweat mingled potently with the smell of poorly cured frontier tobacco. Rezin was on his second ale before he built a cigarette and smoked it in thoughtful silence. A tremendous load—almost a weight—had been lifted off his soul. It was something he'd been carrying for many, many years. The sensation of release made him feel mellow, only dimly aware of the excited talk that was buzzing in the long room. The conversations built around the sudden taking off of Bull Antrim, and the mysterious way in which he had been killed. Enough filtered past his ears, though, to show that no one knew who had been Antrim's killer.

One word—*murder*—kept cropping up, and that made Rezin Hartman's eyes sardonic. Murder wasn't unusual, but it was condemned, especially in a land where every man was foolishly bound by tacit agreement to giving the other fellow an even chance for his life. Rezin laughed inwardly. Antrim was murdered, all right, but not until twenty years after he himself had committed a greater murder.

The ale had a numbing effect. Rezin wondered if Buckrum's law was any better than it had been two decades earlier. He made a small, wry face, then remembered that he had seen a man earlier in the day, wearing a sheriff's star. He caught Frosty's eye. "What's the sheriff's name?"

"Williams. Dexter Williams." Frosty jutted his chin toward the roadway. "Office's across the road."

Rezin nodded, watched the man's back as the barman moved away, and thought to himself: *All right, Dexter Williams, let's see you find the killer.*

• • •

The sheriff was a lean string bean of a man with graying hair, perpetually squinted eyes, and a too-wide mouth. Also, he was a particular, methodical man who rarely moved in anything resembling a hurry. He regarded his deputy unblinkingly and nodded at the worn .44 on his desk without saying a word. Deputy Berl Clausen tossed his head sideways to dislodge a droplet of sweat that hung to the end of his nose.

"Antrim's gun. Two of them the same afternoon. Quite a coincidence, ain't it?"

Dexter Williams nodded again, still silent.

Berl's glance went to the gun. "Got an empty cartridge in it. Under the hammer, and once over. Still stunk, too, when I got there and picked it up."

Dexter's eyes roved over the gun indifferently, then swung back to Berl. "Y'know, Berl, there's times when things seem to move in twos. Y'ever notice that?" He touched the gun with a long, tapered finger. "Like this, for instance. Porky John, the Digger Injun, was shot and killed, and Bull Antrim was shot and killed. Pretty close to the same time of day, too. Now, here's two dead men. In twos, y'see? All right, now then, both of them's been around Buckrum and the Brazitos country for better'n twenty years. But today . . . all of a sudden . . . practically in the same hour . . . they're both shot down. And they're fifteen miles apart when it happens."

Berl wagged his head. "Like I said . . . coincidence."

He eased off one leg on the hard chair, to revive its circulation while the other leg supported his weight. "I got an idea, Dex. If a man could figure out these coincidences, maybe he'd be able to follow them, like a pair of wagon ruts, sort of, and go right to the killers." Berl saw the sheriff's eyes waver as though his thoughts were wandering, and let it drop.

Chapter Two
TWO KINDS OF WOMEN

The shadows were mathematical patterns of blunt squares reflected off the town's buildings opposite the saloon. They had dipped low over the batwing doors, when Conseil Purdy came out of his little office and saw Owl Russel leaning over the bar at the far end, where it joined the wall, holding a whiskey mash in his hand. Purdy's insides contorted a little. He'd heard of the Indian's passing, but had never expected to see the killer again. Gunmen rode in, took their money, killed, and rode out. It made him uneasy.

He flagged the barman with his head, and went over to the small table he kept reserved for himself. Frosty hid the annoyed look in his eyes, made up an ale, and toted it over to his employer in spite of the clamor at the bar. Purdy sipped it without looking back at Owl.

Trade was beginning to come in. In singles, doubles, and mobs of parched, boisterous cowboys, flavored with townsmen, freighters, and travelers. Purdy could see the door from where he sat. He saw Ed Smith come in for his pre-supper beer, and ignored the liveryman.

Owl Russel watched the crowd build up into its full strength with cold eyes. Men seemed to sense his hostility and left him ample elbow room in spite of the cramped condition at the bar. He knew better than to believe it was because of the twin ivory-butted guns. He'd felt it before, in other towns and bars along the frontier. It was some peculiar aura, maybe, that repelled people. At least, it repelled enough people so that he was rarely jostled or accosted.

Owl listened to the talk. It was on the gossip level, except for some riders he knew were CL cowhands by their verbal identification. These men lapped up drinks and retold the tale of their foreman's killing. They were all in the bunkhouse when Antrim had been shot down, and laughed scornfully, derisively, when anyone foolishly asked if they'd seen the gunman. No, they hadn't. Furthermore, no one in his right mind would poke a head out a door under the circumstances, either. Not when he didn't know what was waiting outside.

There was some casual mention of the dead Digger, too. But it was soon forgotten in the more savory killing of Bull Antrim. Owl was pleased at that, although he really didn't care. Someone in the jostling crowd poked a thoughtless elbow into his kidneys from behind. He turned with a livid curse, reached out, and caught the first man handy, yanked him in close, and slashed out with his open hand. It happened to be an old man known as Deacon Will. He banged into the packed bodies, arms flailing, then went down into the filthy sawdust, and lay there. He looked up in a bewildered, cringing way. Quaking fingers dabbed at the lacing of blood that trickled from his left ear. Owl glared down, but inside he felt almost sick over the blow. There was something child-like in the old man's eyes. Owl didn't know it—and never found out—but the oldster was the single survivor of a massacred host of immigrants. He had never recovered from the horrors of his experience. Men called him Deacon Will because all he knew about himself was that his name was Will something or other. The Deacon had become attached because he was always talking about God and the hereafter.

A hard face loomed over the old man. Owl saw the flaming anger in the blue eyes as the strange cowboy balled his fists. "What's the matter, stranger? Feared to jump someone closer to your own heft?"

The fires of hell and torment had subsided. Owl's fury was past. He gauged the cowboy, saw trouble coming that couldn't be avoided, and lashed out a second time. Bystanders fought each other to get clear. The big cowboy went over sideways, caught himself, and roared a rain of curses. His lips were bared. Owl waited until he was close enough, then kicked out hard with his pointed toe. The spur rang wildly when his foot connected with the pelvic bone. The cowboy screamed in agony and doubled over. Owl stepped over closer to the wall, watching the man. No one said anything, but raw hate was heavy in the air. He motioned to a Mexican standing nearby.

"Drag him outside."

The Mexican had hard work of it. The cowboy was doubled over into a knot of dead weight. Too, he was almost twice as heavy as the Mexican, but there was an incentive: Owl Russel's rabid face. The Mexican grunted and tugged through an opening among the patrons, followed unsteadily by the blank-eyed old man known as Deacon Will.

Con Purdy had seen the whole thing, and his nervousness was heightened by it. He chewed the senseless flesh inside his face until he thought of something. There was a sallow young man at the piano. Purdy nodded to him, and music broke over the hush like weak, soothing syrup. Gradually the Parker House Saloon got back almost to normal. Owl Russel felt the hostile stares, though, and his antagonism toward all men came back stronger. They were like sheep. Fifty or more to one, and they let it slide. He stared woodenly at the night barman and nodded at his empty glass. The man grabbed it up for a refill.

"Yellow buzzards," Owl Russel said softly yet audibly.

The music brought a large woman to the partition doorway that separated the card room from the saloon proper. She threw a glance over the men and leaned against the wall, and started to sing, watching the effect. It was immediate and electric. The noise died to a low hum. Owl Russel looked surprised, and stared.

He differed from the others in many things, but not in his hungers.

The singer's name was Liza Bent. She was a big girl with black hair and eyes to match. Her features weren't coarse, but they were large. She had a way of looking with scorn over the heads of the men that excited Owl. He knew the luxury of arrogance and liked it in this big woman. There was something unusual about the way her eyes swept upward at their outer corners that was a portent to him. Indian blood. He also liked that.

Liza ended her song, turned scoffingly at the men's shouts, and almost—not quite—went back into the card room. Con Purdy threw a handful of silver dollars at her. It was a put-up and well timed. The cowmen and freighters caught on, stamped their feet until the tiny music of spur rowels and thick-soled boots made dull thunder, and threw cartwheels and adobe dollars at her feet. She waited until the silver rain subsided, motioned an Indian girl forward with a hand basket to receive the money, then strolled, rolling her hips, farther into the saloon, singing.

Owl Russel saw the whole act. The way Purdy threw the coins that started the avalanche, and the way she treated the men like they were beneath her, and admired it for what it was, because he, also, held men—and most women—in contempt. The black eyes of the man followed the girl's body with every movement. Some kind of a red spark, invisible but tangible, nonetheless, went past the others to her. She looked around until her eyes came to Owl Russel's glance, flitted on, stopped on the wall, and came back. He didn't smile or laugh, or shout encouragement, like the others, but his message was direct and understood. Liza Bent looked at him askance, saw the dark vigor in his face, and the handsomeness of his breadth, height, and looks, and liked what she saw, too.

Owl straightened over the bar, draped his elbows on either side of him, and watched the woman. She didn't fail to notice his standing among the men. Normally men would challenge anyone's right to so much room at the bar on a crowded night. That the others left the stranger strictly alone was proof of his standing. She traded stare for stare. Liza was a big girl who liked big men. The stranger was big.

When Liza's song ended the second time, the men catcalled at her. She ignored them until two Texans converged on her with loud shouts of admiration. Her stare at Owl Russel was broken by two faded shirts and bronzed faces that flashed white teeth and knowing looks. Owl pushed off the bar, shoved through the press of humanity, and made his way toward the girl. She saw him coming, but the Texans didn't. Their backs were to him. He elbowed both of them away. One lost himself in the crowd readily enough, but the other hesitated, giving glare for glare. Owl's cauldron simmered. He swore gently at the man. The rider's face whitened. Owl's cursing began to assume comprehensive dimensions. It swept over the man's mother, his father, his legitimacy and, finally, his courage. There was something crawling under Russel's skin again. This time under circumstances that were far better. He dared the Texan to fight, reviled him, and reveled in it because the stake was the woman behind him.

The cowboy suddenly shook his head from side to side wildly, straightened up, turned with almost a sob, and hastened out of the saloon. Buckrum lost a visitor that night. Owl turned, let the venom of his eyes rake the watchers, read dread in a lot of faces, and swung his eyes away contemptuously to Liza Bent.

"Over there. That table by the stove."

He walked abruptly away. Liza followed. They sat down under the heady realization that furtive eyes were watching them. They both liked it that way. Owl enjoyed the woman's desirability among the men even as she savored his mastery among the others. They were a lot alike. Owl flagged the barman and ordered drinks. They came quickly enough, and Conseil Purdy chewed the lining of his face as he watched the gunman and his hired singer.

"What's your name?"

"Liza Bent. What's yours?"

"Owl Russel."

"Stranger to Buckrum?"

"Yeah. Just rode in."

"Traveling through?"

Owl shook his head significantly, staring at her. "No. Reckon not. I've just seen something here I like. I'm going to stay for a while." When she didn't say anything, he sipped his mash and watched her drink the watered whiskey. "I like music. Always did. I like the way you sing 'Gary Owen'."

Liza smiled. Her teeth were large and even. It was hard to define the peculiar feeling she had about this man with the dual ivory-gripped guns, but it wasn't unpleasant.

"You think of some special song and I'll sing it for you tomorrow night."

"Not before?"

She started to explain that she only sang once a night, then clamped her jaw closed. She understood the innuendo. "No," she said decisively. She meant it two ways, and Owl understood it that way. He kept his eyes on her face, forcing them to stay up there. He didn't want her to know what he was thinking—yet. His lips curled a little at their outer edges, but the black eyes remained blank.

"Awright. Come on. I need some fresh air. Go out onto the walk with me."

He didn't wait for an answer or give her a chance to make one. He got up and started for the doors. Liza watched his broad back, the way it flared outward from the waist, got up, and followed him through the crowd. They were both conscious of the stares that followed them. The limelight was like opium to them both. Liza tossed her head at the sardonic little smile on the cowboy with the bronze-gold hair at a small table near the doorway, with an older man, sitting slumped over, beside him.

Rezin watched them go with a hard little smile. His Uncle Burt didn't see either Owl or the girl. His thoughts weren't anywhere near the Parker House Saloon. Liza was last through the louvered opening. Rezin's eyes raked her once, then swung back to the table. He hunched forward a little and stared down into his ale. It had lost its tang, but he didn't like whiskey.

Uncle Burt sat slouched, pressing his blunt, padded fingers against tired eyelids. "None of them recognized you, Rezin." Hunt's voice sounded amazed. "You did it, and there's the end to it. Now go back up north and forget the whole damned thing. You've got the money I put in trust for you. Buy a good little ranch and forget the Brazitos." He looked over at the younger man. "It's cost me dear, boy, to see you educated and taught the cowman's trade. But it was worth it. Up to now, anyway. I only had one sister, Rezin. You're her only kid. I don't grudge you a cent of what it's cost me. My family don't know anything about it, either." He slouched backwards in the chair. "Just let it stand that the last of the Hartmans came back and squared an old debt. Just you and me'll ever know."

Rezin looked up. "How about the land my folks scrabbled into a ranch, Burt? I'm supposed to let that go, too?"

Hunt was beginning to feel a sense of futility in what he was trying to do. He didn't give up, though. "Listen to me, Rezin. Like I said earlier, I'm older. I know how useless it is for a man to spend himself warring.

89

I know that one killing always begets another one until the man that's done the warring can't get out. Until he gets killed, too." He was propped on the table himself now, leaning over toward his nephew. There was desperation and appeal in his eyes. "Don't try to make it *all* up, Rezin. Let the past have it. That's where it belongs, anyway. All of it. You're just so much ahead now. You're as far ahead, boy, as Antrim is a long way off. Nothing'll bring Birch and Tamsen Hartman back to us, son. Nothing. But you'll go and join them if you ride off wild on a hate trail, Rezin. That's gospel, boy."

Rezin didn't answer. The crystal-clear hardness of his lifelong lust for vengeance let him have a fleeting glance of Burt Hunt's side of it. Burt was past sixty. He was composing himself—whether he knew it or not—for greater rewards. He had the sluggish blood of age that turned vigor to thoughtfulness, tinted with a certain defeatism, an insidious fatalism that refused to get involved with earth's tangents and viciousness.

Rezin Hartman wasn't sixty. His blood was fast-flowing and free. He had lived too long with the fixed intention of avenging his murdered parents. The law never had, and his only living relative wouldn't. Therefore, it became his duty, his own, private hate trail.

"No, Burt, if even a half-hearted investigation had been made, if anyone'd tried to get to the bottom of it. . . ." He glanced up with an intent look. "If just any one of the people who'd said they were friends had done something, I might feel different. But the Brazitos acted like dead Hartmans were welcome." His anger filled him, in spite of an heroic effort to keep it down. "Now the men who did the killing are going to learn something." The fury held him solidly in its grip. His blue eyes flamed. Burt Hunt saw the look and knew it wasn't something that could be overcome with two drinks of ale. It had been too many years getting entrenched and set in the man's system. His heart sank a little. He knew there was trouble ahead, violent, bloody trouble, and he fervently wanted to keep his sister's son out of it and alive. He couldn't and knew it, in that moment, because Rezin Hartman himself *was* the trouble.

Burt felt all used up inside. He was picking words carefully in his mind and arranging them for a final appeal when a scream rent the air. It had a wild, abandoned awfulness to it that rose and fell with choking sobs that made the blood run cold. He was petrified by the sound, like the rest of the men in the Parker House Saloon were.

The doors burst inward and quivered. Liza Bent ran staggeringly into the room. A livid bruise stood out on her cheek where the back of an angry hand had struck her. Glassy-eyed, the girl ran up the stairs to the balcony overhead.

Rezin saw the girl rush past, and swung his eyes, still wild and fiery, back to the doorway. Owl Russel rammed into the room hurling epithets after her. His face was sweaty and contorted. A long, angry slash of a fingernail was red and sullen down the side of his thick neck. He was reeling a little, with the flames of hell in his face.

Rezin never remembered crossing the room or leaving Burt Hunt at the table. He saw a bloated, mahogany-colored face loom up before him, insane-eyed and suffused with dark blood. Then he felt his fists pounding hard flesh as he slammed Owl Russel to his knees, kicked him viciously up to his feet again, yanked and whirled him farther into the saloon, and ripped into his flesh with unheeding, insanely furious fists.

Russel went down under the unexpected wildness of the attack. Rezin yanked him upright in a nightmare of hoarse screams and shouts that suddenly filled his world, and lashed out with all his strength. The gunman's body hurtled through the stingy alley of human beings and fetched up, hard against the bar. Dust flew out of the stuffed eagle over the bar, then Rezin was on the partially paralyzed man again, like a panther.

Russel tasted the sour, green bile that erupted into his mouth from his churned stomach and let it trickle past numb lips as instinct drove his rubber fingers to the ivory-butted guns. Rezin slashed murderously at the whiskey-filled stomach, raised his sights slightly, and pounded along the ribs, up higher into the dark face. He threw a final punch with a wild grunt and watched Owl Russel collapse with a shrill sob that let the bile past his lips, when he fell into the spit-encrusted sawdust of the barroom floor.

Conseil Purdy was clawing through the howling mob, panting and swearing. The mighty shout that went up when Owl Russel fell gave him added strength. He pummeled and roared and pushed past the men until he was standing not more than five feet from Rezin Hartman.

"Get out! Get the devil out of here! There'll be no more fightin' in the Parker House. Pick up your hat and clear out!" Purdy was yelling, when suddenly he heard the hush and knew he had been yelling excitely over a tumult that no longer existed. He threw an arm toward the door and lowered his voice. "And don't come back unless you're ready to act different."

Rezin looked callously at the shorter, swarthy man, disconnectedly and irrelevantly guessed him to be a French-Canadian, turned on his heel, retrieved his hat, and at the same moment saw his old table was vacant. He knew Burt had left during the battle. He stalked out into the balmy night, where a high sky was offering weak, watery light from a half moon, and the prismatic beauty of a million stars shone dully on him. He made a wry face at his uncle's desertion and walked stiffly toward the livery barn.

Rezin told Cleat to saddle his grulla, walked out to the water trough, and sluiced water, warmer than the night air, over his face, neck, and arms. It stung the bruised, scored meat of his hands where the flesh had been shredded against buttons, bone, and twin belt buckles. He ran swelling hands through the tousled mop of bronze-gold hair in lieu of a comb, put his hat on, and went back inside. Cleat took the half dollar, shot Rezin a surprised, vague smile, and watched him swing up and ride out of the barn. Rezin turned north until he was clear of Buckrum, then swung south and went like an invincible magnet was drawing him back down the dead land, still warm from the smashing heat of the day.

The abandoned wagon trail was indistinct under the grulla's hoofs, but Rezin followed it easily enough. Finally even the big ridgling got the idea and walked along, reins flopping, following each snaky turn of the all-but-erased ruts, choked and grown over with rank grass and seedling brush. Nature had almost reclaimed her own. The ancient tracks were hidden in the night. In the horseman's memory, though, they were plain enough.

Rezin was far down the CL range that spread out, deep and immense, from Buckrum, north, south, and southwest, before he came once more to the abandoned ranch. The log house and carefully chinked log barn, where the wattles had hardly changed at all in spite of the neglect of several decades, were pale in the moonlight. He rode in through the gaping gate hole in the shattered picket fence, looked around in the moist moonlight for a second, then swung down, unsaddled, hobbled the grulla, and eased off the spade bit. He watched the big animal shake himself luxuriously and hop off toward the smell of water at an overflow seepage from the box spring around the edge of the house. He made a cigarette, lit it, and smoked thoughtfully, without moving, for a long time. Then he spat in his palm, snuffed out the quirly, dropped it, and walked over to the house.

Inside, wood rats, bats, and other small animals had played havoc. Rezin scarcely noticed the rubbish as he walked from room to room. His booted feet made hollow sounds that echoed in the cool darkness. The place was eerily iridescent where the faint light filtered through the empty windows, like sightless eye sockets.

His imagination peopled the house with a sturdily built woman with bronze-gold hair and tolerant, humorous blue eyes. There was a raw-boned man, too, with an auburn beard, laughter wrinkles, a wise, knowing look, and huge hands that had a skill rarely given to one person alone. He saw, also, a curious, wide-eyed boy of eight or nine with the red-gold hair of the woman and the indomitable jaw, and the fine, icy blue eyes of the man.

Rezin's thoughts were dim and hazy, but he heard the laughter of these people over by the fireplace, at night after supper, and he also heard some squalling shrieks when the strong woman applied a willow switch for infractions. He turned back and went outside, rolled another cigarette, and dragged the saddle, bridle, and blanket over to the boxed-in spring around the corner of the house. He dumped them there, pulled another blanket from behind the cantle, made up an adequate pallet, lay down, and smiled while the immensity of the night overhead wrapped him in its infinite mystery. He pushed out the second cigarette, kicked off the spurred boots, rolled onto his side, and slept.

Rezin Hartman's body had burned a lot of energy, a tremendous amount, in fact. It had to be replaced. He slept until the sun was navel high off the horizon and warming up for its full blast of summer rage. He awoke with fresh sweat starting out over him, got up, skimmed the twigs and leaves off the spring, stripped, and bathed in the icy spring water until his teeth chattered, rubbed himself dry, and dressed.

He shaved, using the settled water as a mirror, rolled and broke his camp, ate out of the saddlebags, and was walking around in front of the old house again when he saw the sign. It was hand-painted in bold, black letters, and stated bluntly:

NO TRESPASSING.
KEEP OUT.
PRIVATE PROPERTY.
CL RANCH.
TRESPASSERS WILL BE PROSECUTED.
CLIFF LEWIS

Rezin's lips curled. He reached up, got a firm hold of the edge, and pulled. The sign came loose and fell with two small sounds. He kicked the thing away so that it lay, broken and face up, in the trampled grass. His spurs rang as he went back around the house, finished his smoke, and scooped up some of the cold spring water for a drink. It was the best water in the Brazitos. He'd heard men say that twenty years ago.

Rezin was still tasting the spring water with the appreciation of a man who values the precious things of the earth, his hands cupped to his mouth, when a voice sent his back muscles tense with apprehension.

"What're you doing here?"

Rezin relaxed gradually. It was a woman's voice, although the tone was anything but pleasant. He turned slowly, drying his hands on his shirt front. She was a tall, clean-limbed thing on a chestnut mare with a flaxen mane and tail. He looked up at the green eyes framed in the flushed, perspiring face, with its small nose saddled with tiny freckles, and recognized beauty.

Her legs were long, lithe, but fully rounded in the tight old Levi's. Her hair was gathered rather carelessly behind her, beneath a soft Stetson with a flat crown that was furry with the dust. A green ribbon held her hair severely.

He was watching the cupid's-bow lips, parted a little over her small, white teeth, when he answered. "Just relaxing a little, miss."

The green eyes were cold, with a hint of arrogance. It amused him even though it also pricked his soul a little, too. "You're trespassing, cowboy. Drifters aren't allowed to camp on the CL. This land is posted." Her head swung sideways, toward the house, and one gloved hand pointed. "This. . . ." She stopped, glanced from the darker blot of log wall where the sign had been, to the ground where it lay broken, face up, near her horse. The hand jerked back and rested on the swells of her saddle. The green eyes were blazing now. She nodded toward the sign in the grass without looking away from him.

"Did you do that?"

Rezin nodded somberly. "Yes'm."

"Why? Don't you respect the rights of others?"

Two little marks of color appeared in his blank face under the blue eyes. "You wouldn't understand, miss."

"No?" she snapped. "You'll understand something pretty quick." She was reining around as she spoke. "You'll learn not to molest other people's property when I get back home and tell my father a . . . a . . . drifter"—she spat it out with vast contempt—"deliberately tore down one of our signs."

Rezin nodded gently. "Then you must be a Lewis?"

"I am. I'm Faith Lewis. My father's Cliff Lewis, owner of the CL." She rode out through the gate hole, rigid and red with outrage. "You'll have about half an hour, maybe a little more, to get off CL land. If you're not off by then, the boys'll find you. Then you'll learn respect for the CL."

Rezin's spurs sang softly as he walked swiftly forward, half across the weedy yard. "If you're Cliff Lewis's daughter, miss, you can carry a message to him for me." He was stung angry.

She hesitated, twisted sideways, and leaned over the cantle with one hand on the chestnut mare's rump. It forced her upper body into a protruding profile. He saw and noticed.

"What?"

"Tell him Birch Hartman's boy is back. Tell him Antrim got what he had coming to him. Tell him I'll look him up one of these days, too."

Faith Lewis froze in her saddle. The anger disappeared and horror filled its place. Her mouth was partly open. "You . . . you're the one . . . the man . . . that killed Bull?"

Rezin nodded coldly. "Yes'm. An eye for an eye. Your dad'll know what I mean." He waved contemptuously at the broken sign. "He'll understand why I tore down that sign, too. Murderers may escape the law. God knows they do often enough. But there's one law that won't give up. Tell him that, miss, and watch his face. If he gets white around the jaws, you'll have your proof that he knows what a murderer feels. If he doesn't . . . why, then, just send your CL riders on over. Maybe I'll still be here."

He turned abruptly and walked back around the corner of the house. He was more angry at himself for saying things that would put Cliff Lewis on his guard than he was at the girl for her anger-inciting attitude.

Faith Lewis watched him disappear around the old house, shook out her reins, and turned back in the saddle, stunned and horrified that she had just been face to face with the CL foreman's killer.

• • •

Even the morning sun that made her chestnut mare's coat a dark scarlet passed unnoticed as Faith Lewis rode the long trail around Razorback toward the home ranch. She was badly shaken. The stark suddenness of Antrim's killing in the very dooryard of the CL, biggest, most powerful cow outfit in the Brazitos, had stirred up a hornets' nest. It was the first time she'd ever seen a dead man up close.

The fact that Faith had known Bull all her life and had seen him loaded into the buckboard for his last trip to Buckrum didn't alter her feelings any more than her quiet dislike for his brutality with horses and cattle. It had been an awful blow, and now she'd been face to face with his killer, read anger in the blue eyes, and seen determination in the cant of the blunt jaw as well.

She was pale when she swung down by the corrals and loosened the mare's cinch, after tying her in the shade of a shaggy old oak. The frank appreciation in the riders' eyes as they nodded and smiled at her when she walked past was scarcely noticed.

She saw Heber Kimball just leaving the verandah after talking with her father, who was sitting in a cane-bottomed chair tugging at his boots, iron-gray hair sticking up all awry in spite of the water he'd slavered over it.

Heber touched his hat and smiled. Faith nodded, but just couldn't force up a smile. The new foreman looked a little surprised, but walked on by without a word, heading for where the boys were clustered by the corral.

Cliff Lewis was a man so used to power that he wore it with an unconsciousness that was graceful. His moustache was snow-white and always a little unkempt and wind-blown. The face was burned bronze color and usually impassive, aloof and mahogany-colored in its aged majesty.

Faith was looking at him in a new light. He'd been both father and mother to her, and she knew him as a hard man. Now, though, she searched the hard face, with its overtones of fairness, for ruthlessness. Her new perspective saw smoothed-over hints of shriveled emotions that once had made him greatly feared and respected. There was a subtle patience to Cliff, like that of a shaggy lobo wolf. It meant he'd wait forever, but never give up until he conquered. He was massive and thick-bodied, with large, work-swollen hands and a barrel chest above a flat stomach. He smiled as she came up onto the verandah.

"Out early, aren't you, honey?"

"Dad." He heard the flatness of her tone and looked up from tugging at a stubborn boot, graved with a silver inlaid Chihuahua spur. "Dad, I just met a man who said he killed Bull Antrim. He said you'd hear from him soon. He was. . . ."

"Where?" The boot went on with a spasmodic jerk of the powerful arms and shoulders that made the seams give a little.

"He was over at the old Hartman place. He said

101

you'd know how a murderer felt. He was camping there. He pulled down. . . ."

"Hartman!" Lewis was on his feet, the roar that came out of him carrying to the startled cowboys down by the corrals. His face was ashen. He seemed to weave a little as he stared at his daughter. "Hartman!"

The sudden, stricken look on her father's face made Faith force the words that were imprisoned under her tongue to lie there. She recalled the stranger's words: *If he gets white around the jaws. . . .* She couldn't speak. Her throat was a tight knot of hard gristle. Cliff Lewis's face suddenly filled with blood again. He brushed past Faith and hastened toward his riders. He was muttering something to himself, but she couldn't understand. She sank down in the old chair he'd vacated, and watched as Heber Kimball frowned and went a few steps away from the other men to meet him.

"Heber, I'll take the boys with me. You ride to Buckrum for Dexter Williams. By God, there's some buzzard camping over at the old Hartman place who told Faith he killed Bull. Get to horse, man, and bring Dex back to the Hartman place as fast as you can." He went into the barn, reappeared in an instant with his coiled lariat, and stalked toward the corralled horses, shaking out an angry loop. "We'll entertain this gunman until you and Dex get there, Heber. Get going!"

The CL's new foreman mounted the horse he had

saddled before breakfast and spun out of the yard in a long, smooth lope. His shocked face was pale under the beaver belly color of his Stetson. Faith watched him go with a sinking sensation. There would be a fight, sure, unless the stranger was gone. She doubted very much that he would be, before her father and the four riders, who were trotting, stiff-legged, out of the yard at that instant, got to the abandoned ranch.

On a sudden impulse, Faith Lewis jumped out of the chair and raced to the little chestnut mare, gave the cinch a nervous tug, piled aboard, and swung around, riding out of the yard directly toward Razorback. She leaned forward in her saddle and patted the powerful neck.

"I'm sorry, Gelita. It'll be awfully hard on you. But if we don't go over Razorback, instead of around it like the boys did, there'll be a killing. I'm sure of it. We've got to stop it." She thought of the stranger. He had a certain look that went with two guns, and he also had the guns. She felt the mare strain into the talus and loose lava rock. Her father had said—"Hartman!"— like it was a curse, and, having seen the gunman, she could sense that his being here *was* a curse.

Rezin had caught the grulla, sponged his salty back at the spring, loafed until the hair was dry, saddled up and bridled the animal. He was eating a meager dinner of sardines from a flat can when he heard the horse coming hell for leather down the land. He finished eating, tossed the can toward the ancient refuse pile around the edge of the house, and listened with a frown as the drumming hoof beats swept closer.

He was dumbfounded when she spun in through the old gate and slid to an earth-churning halt that flung pebbles over him. He fished out his tobacco sack and papers and deliberately went to work, swinging one leg from the perch he had on the side of the box spring. His knowing eye took in the used-up look of the chestnut mare. Caustically he nodded his head.

"I see you're as disagreeable with horses as you are with people." He flicked a light, sucked in the smoke, and snapped the match. "Being cruel must run in the blood." He read the tension in her face.

"You . . . you've got to ride!" Faith's eyes were wide with premonition over what she had unleashed. "My father's coming. He. . . ."

"Fine. That'll save me hunting him down." The spurred boot still swung lazily back and forth.

"No, listen! I was a fool. To tell him, I mean. He's got four of the cowboys with him, and he's fighting mad. There'll be trouble." She leaned far over, sideways from the saddle, pleading with him. "Please, cowboy. . . ."

"My name's Rezin Hartman, Miss Lewis." He canted his head toward the bleached log house. "I was born here."

"Mister Hartman, go! Ride for it! Don't stay. Someone'll be hurt . . . killed, maybe."

"Yeah. It won't be the first time in this place, miss. Maybe a murderer'll die here. I hope so."

"Mister Hartman, it couldn't have been my dad. He. . . ."

"How'd he look when you told him about me? A little shook up and white, maybe? A little scared?" His cold blue eyes were flashing fire at her.

She shook her head and lied—poorly. "No. He . . . he looked mad, is all. Just mad."

Rezin shook his head, spat into his hand, and snuffed out the cigarette. "You're not a good liar, Miss Lewis. Miss Faith Lewis," he added.

"Can't you see? Nothing good can come of you facing five armed men here . . . now! Please! Oh, please, Mister Hartman, ride. Go away. I'll . . . I'll find out the truth for you." It was a dazzlingly sudden inspiration, prompted by desperation. "Better than you can, too. Really I can. I swear I will. Give me until tomorrow, but don't stay and kill someone, or be killed." She looked behind her, over where the faint trail swept around the edge of Razorback. The land shimmered in vacant loneliness except for some tail-swishing cattle in the near distance.

Rezin was very calm. He admired her *retroussée* profile when she looked around. His mind wasn't on vengeance, especially, just then, but her next words brought him sharply back to it.

"Mister Hartman, if you'll trust me, I'll find out the truth for you. Will you give me the chance?" The green eyes were begging and compelling at the same time. "I . . . I've got to know, too."

He looked up at her, the way she was unconsciously

and fervently bent forward over the mare's neck. He got off the box spring, walked over close, reached up impulsively, grasped both her shoulders, pulled her savagely forward and downward a little. Rezin bluntly put his mouth over the moist, startled softness of her lips, let go roughly, and stepped back with a brick-red face.

Faith Lewis was too stunned to speak until after he had swung up into the saddle, kneed in close beside her, and was looking down into her green eyes with a cruel stare.

"All right, miss. I'll give you the time you want . . . until tomorrow at dawn . . . to get the whole story of the killing of Tamsen and Birch Hartman. Bring it to me, here." He started to rein past, looked down the trail around Razorback, and saw the shimmering blot of bunched riders coming, small yet, and let his words drift back over his shoulder to her. "I don't think you'll be able to find out in twenty hours, or so, what's been a mystery for that many years, though." He rode out through the broken gate without a backward glance and kicked the grulla up into an easy lope, heading northeast, around the upper end of Razorback.

He didn't hear her begin a protest that it was dangerous to meet him here, at the old Hartman place, the following dawn. If he had, he wouldn't have changed his plans, anyway. There was a certain bitter satisfaction, to Rezin, in thinking he would make the old ranch, so lonely and deserted, inhabited again in the final act of justice against the murderers of his people.

Faith watched him go with roiled emotions. Twenty-one years of life hadn't created the turbulence that had sprung, full grown, to worry her in the past five hours. She sat perfectly still and saw the dark blot become her father and the four CL riders. They were all armed to the teeth and mounted on good, breedy CL horses. The sight had always made her proud, but today the heat waves that made them dance like they were actually riding a few inches off the ground also made her look at them in awe, tinctured with a little fear.

Cliff Lewis had hired his men through the years for their hard capabilities. These included iron loyalty to the brand they rode for, a certain hardness that made CL cowboys known and respected across the territory, which upheld the prestige of his mighty empire of grass and cattle, and the riders' willingness to wear and use guns in the furtherance of CL range domination.

The four men coming along behind Lewis were typical of the men he had always hired, lean, hard, capable and willing, but not inhuman or cold. Faith's pride came back up again, but the little hint of fear didn't leave. She was looking at her father's men—and old Cliff as well—in the same light, without knowing it, that most of the Brazitos countrymen did.

She watched Cliff's arm raise and point toward the distant rider. Quickly she appraised the distance, and knew her father wouldn't order a chase. The sun would kill a running horse in short order. She swung back when someone shouted, saw her father turn back onto the old trail, and ride directly toward where she sat by the old log house. Her heart sank, but there was no retreat from what she had done. The main thing was that she'd prevented a fight, a killing, possibly. She looked around. Rezin Hartman was small in the distance, and still riding.

Rezin checked the grulla ridgling when he saw the CL riders swing back onto the established trail and ride slowly toward the Hartman place. He looked past them to the waiting rider in the trampled yard. She had done a rash thing. The consequences were somber enough. She'd have to face her father. He swung back in the saddle, unconsciously eyeing the vastness of the uninhabited land, and thought of Faith Lewis.

Strangely his mind made a sudden comparison between her and Liza Bent. His lips curled sardonically. They had two things in common. Both were abundantly feminine, and both had fire, but, beyond that, the abyss widened and widened until more than caste and origin and environment separated them.

He looked down at the grulla's small ears. "Two different kinds of women," he said. The horse batted his ears, then ignored the sound. He was accustomed to having his rider talk to himself, after the fashion of all men much alone.

Chapter Three
THE GATHERING STORM

Berl Clausen got back to the sheriff's office first. He dumped a battered six-gun onto the desk, blew out a ragged, relieved breath, and kicked his chair up against the wall, studied it critically, and sat down, gingerly leaning back and hooking his boots over the lowest rung. The chair gave out no ominous skidding sounds.

Berl slung his head sideways abruptly to shake off the tenacious droplet of sweat that clung to his nose, reached for the plug of Day's Work, worried off a small piece, tongued it up into the pouch of his cheek, and relaxed. His job had been the simplest. He knew that was why Dex had sent him over to the coroner's. Bull Antrim had been killed by an unidentified gunman, apparently because of some feud. No one seemed to mourn his passing.

Berl let his eyelids droop in the coolness of the office. He was drowsing contentedly when the door swung open, and Dexter stumped in. He looked over at the sheriff, saw the damp coil of long hair around the prominent ears, and waited.

Sheriff Williams tossed a careless glance at Berl, at the worn gun on his desk, cast his hat to the deer-horn rack, and plumped into his cane-bottomed chair with a loud sigh.

"Gawd! Must be a hundred and twenty out."

Berl didn't answer.

Dexter made a sloppy cigarette and plugged it into his mouth listlessly. His glance fell solemnly to the gun on his desk. "Anything new?"

"No. Just like we figured. Killed by an unidentified party, or parties. That's all. Didn't see a tear in the place. Doc says he'll plant him in the new cemetery."

Dex grunted, squirmed in the chair, and exhaled. "The old one's best for his kind."

Berl nodded agreeably. "Yeah, but it's about filled up to overflowing." He shrugged. "Antrim'll be lonely in the new one. Haven't been many hawks buried there. Brazitos has been growing up since the new one got started. Progress, I reckon. Country's quieting down."

Again Dexter snorted. "Progress, huh? Well . . . maybe. But it's sure balking lately. No gunfights for three months, then . . . bang! . . . two killings in one day."

"You do any good?"

Dexter shook his head. "Like this. The Digger woman's gone. Even the goats aren't there any more. There's a grave beside the shack is all." His somber eyes went over Berl's head to the blank wall where, in idle moments, he traced out designs among the fly specks, like some people do in the stars at night. "I reckon she's gone back to her people. Anyway, there's no reason for her to hang around no longer. Old Digger Porky John wasn't a bad Injun. Can't figure why anyone'd bother to kill him. He hardly even drank. Worked for a lot of cowmen, off and on, too. Never heard anyone say much against him."

Berl looked impatient. "How about suspects?" He shook off sweat with an annoyed shake of his head. "Other Injuns maybe, or strangers?"

Dexter grunted. "Not Injuns. I'll bet on that."

"Well . . . strangers, then. There's a dozen new faces in town. Some of those freighters, maybe. . . ."

Dexter shrugged. "Maybe. There's some gunmen in town, too."

Berl nodded shortly. "Yeah. There's a light-haired one I seen. He darned near skinned a 'breed two-gun man alive at the Parker House last night, they tell me."

"Not him, Berl. He just don't fit. Or . . . if he does, I'm a poor judge of men. Anyway . . . what in tarnation would a high-priced gunman kill an Injun for, anyway? Porky John was nothing."

Berl nodded absently. "How about the other one?"

Dex's eyes came down off the wall and narrowed just a tiny bit. "Disagreeable buzzard, that feller. I'm glad I wasn't there last night when he got the hell whaled out of him. I'd've had to stop it. He was pretty well patched up. In fact, from what I heard this morning, I expected to find him in bed at the doctor's . . . but he was at the Parker House. He had a sort of used-up look all right, but, besides some pretty ugly gashes on his face, he seemed about the same." Williams dropped the cigarette into a greenish, slippery spittoon beside the desk. "The man can drink liquor. Frosty told me on the sly that he was on his third whiskey mash this morning. Steady, though."

"What's he say?" Berl prompted.

"About what I expected. I asked him about signing a complaint, and he gave me a fishy look for about five seconds before he said anything, then he says . . . 'I take care of my own troubles, Sheriff. You mind your own business and I'll mind mine.'"

Berl's eyes got a tawny look in them.

Dexter went on. "I told him any trouble in Buckrum *was* my business, and, if he'd sign a complaint for assault, I'd run this other one down and lock him up for a while."

"So?"

"So he looks at me with that funny, slow way he has, seems to be considering which nasty crack to make, then just picks up his drink and walks to the other end of the bar and turns his back on me."

Berl sighed. "He's a first-class son-of-a-bitch. I know the type."

"Sure," Dexter agreed. "But you can't arrest a man for what he is. It's what he does that counts." He reached up and scratched the jungle of his sweat-matted hair. "Con sure acts funny around him. Next time you're in the saloon, watch the way Con looks at him."

Berl nodded that he would, and said: "Brought Antrim's gun back after the hearing."

Williams nodded without picking the thing up. "I wonder who the other two-gun man is? The one that kicked hell out of this 'breed?"

"No telling. As long as they war with each other, things'll be fine. Antrim was scum, too, but he sure as hell wasn't in their class."

Dexter leaned forward, fished in a carelessly half-opened bottom drawer, and brought out two muddy bottles of tepid ale. "Berl, we've earned a free drink for this morning. I've been treasuring these for a week or so. Here." He tossed one to the deputy and began to worry the imprisoned cork with his Case knife. Another stupid fly that had blundered into a spider's web was buzzing frenziedly, trying to escape.

Dexter and his deputy savored the bitter ale in dull silence. Berl put his empty bottle on the floor and got up. The sheriff looked at him.

"Where you going?"

"Parker House. Want to look over this 'breed gunman."

The sheriff drained his ale, got up, and felt for his hat. He remembered Antrim's gun and absently shoved it into a drawer.

"I'll go with you."

When they sauntered into the saloon, Owl Russel was up against the wall at the south end of the bar, morosely toying with his drink, twisting it in ever larger circles in its own pool of stickiness.

The saloon was empty except for the day bartender, Frosty, and three old men in a distant corner playing blackjack. Frosty had a sour, damp bar rag folded flat, and was slapping at flies with it. Owl watched his practiced aim dully, then spoke, ignoring the lawmen.

"Where's Liza?"

The barman answered without looking around. "In her room, I reckon. Third door to the left off the upstairs landing."

"This sure is lousy liquor you put in these drinks."

Berl and Dexter Williams exchanged wry looks, but Frosty didn't reply. His life was spent on the fringe of brawls, and he knew when to talk and when not to. Mostly when not to.

"Charge too much, too." There was only the damp *splat* of the bar rag striking at the flies. Owl finished the drink and put the glass down thoughtfully. "Sure made a fool of myself last night, didn't I?"

Frosty couldn't be baited on that line. He'd learned, long ago, that any man who condemned himself objected to agreement on the score. He just shrugged, looked at the empty glass, and raised his eyebrows.

"Another one?"

Owl eyed the glass sourly. "No. Not now. That's what threw me last night. The buzzard caught me half drunk. Otherwise, he'd be in that hearse the liveryman drove up to boothill a few minutes ago, the one carrying that Antrim *hombre* everyone's so glad to see buried."

"Well, how about an ale to settle the liquor?"

"No, don't like the stuff."

Dexter, ignoring the gunman as Owl Russel was ignoring the lawmen, nodded. "Couple of ales here, Frosty."

The barman served them with a half smile showing,

wry and subtle. He said nothing, and turned back to the fly-swatting chore. He looked up, though, when a door opened and closed, saw Conseil Purdy come out of the office, and watched for the familiar jerk of the boss' head, didn't get it, and resumed searching for the diminishing supply of prey.

Berl was sipping his ale, eyeing Owl Russel, but Dexter turned slightly and watched Purdy drop onto the bench at his pet table. Owl saw this, too, and there was a cold smile in his black eyes. Berl watched the man, fascinated. Owl looked like he knew something about Purdy. He did, but Berl couldn't know it for sure. Berl knew the Parker House owner was nervous and uneasy when he saw the gunman watching him. Something else, too, that Owl Russel knew, eased down out of Owl's memory to his thoughts. It didn't amuse him, but it was still ironically true. Maybe, someday, he'd tell Purdy. He shoved off the bar and walked leisurely over toward Con Purdy.

The lawmen listened to his spurs tinkle in the dead atmosphere and looked into his face. They didn't see anything there, though, that augured trouble—just the ruddy, vicious look of any—and all—killers.

Dexter, sensing something, nudged Berl and moved down the bar to where he could watch Purdy's table without having to do it so obviously. The deputy followed, and saw the tight look on Purdy's face when the saloon owner saw the gunman approaching. He seemed to flatten back against the wall. Distaste and fear were in his eyes. Owl didn't sit down on the empty bench across from Purdy. He preferred looking down at men to staring at them from equal eye level.

The words floated easily enough through the silence when Owl spoke. "You know that *hombre* who floored me last night?"

Purdy shook his head vigorously. "No. Never saw him before. He come in just ahead of you."

"He must've left the country. I've been all over town looking for him. No one knows who he was or where he went. His horse's gone from Smith's barn, too."

Something Conseil Purdy had overlooked in the excitement of the last twenty-four hours burst into the front of his mind with a staggering jolt. The stranger with the red-gold hair had been at a table with old Burt Hunt! Purdy's eyes widened on Owl's dark face, looking through it and past, down a series of lurid yesterdays. Another facet slid down beside the first one. The stranger's ice-blue eyes and the bronze-gold hair!

"Jeeze!" It was a blasted whisper backgrounded in pure horror. Berl and Dexter heard it easily and grew intent. Neither had ever seen Con Purdy so excited. Their eyes were glued to the man's glistening face, while an awful thought made Purdy almost cower.

He had had Digger killed because the man was known to have been found and raised by the Hartmans, but Con Purdy had never suspected that the Indian knew anything because he hadn't actually seen the murders, and Purdy had felt secure enough until, two months before, Porky John was seen digging around the graves of the Hartmans.

This report, by casual barroom conversation from idling CL riders, had startled Purdy. It had preyed on his mind. Maybe the Digger had known something, after all. The fact that the killings had occurred two decades before, and the Indian had never spoken of them, made no difference. Purdy was no gambler, never had been, and thus Porky John had been killed. This thought, however, was secondary.

The icy shaft that had sliced into his entrails now brought back the full force of the old fear tenfold. The Digger hadn't talked—so far as he knew. Now, he never would. But this two-gun man with the Hartman eyes and bronze-gold hair. Good God! He'd been sitting with Tamsen Hartman's brother, old Burt Hunt. He must be—had to be—the little kid that had been visiting his cousins in Buckrum the day the Hartmans had been killed.

Purdy's hands were shaking so badly that he put them into his pockets, out of sight, and motioned for Owl to sit down opposite him. The gunman neither obeyed nor acknowledged that he had seen the movement. Purdy's swarthy face was ashen under the oily hide. Owl noticed it and wondered, as also did Dexter Williams and Berl Clausen.

"Maybe he's gone. Maybe he left after you were larruped." Purdy's mind refuted it with irony as he said it. He looked back at Owl again and leaned forward in urgency, lowering his voice so the sheriff couldn't hear him. "But I don't give a damn whether he's gone or not. He's got to be killed. You got to find him and kill him before . . . anyone talks to him. Two thousand, gold, for him dead."

Owl blinked quickly, but his face remained blank. Two thousand was the going price for four killings. Even a territorial governor wasn't worth more than five hundred dead. His tongue darted out, circuited the thin lips, and ducked back into the moist lair.

"Get it."

Dexter watched Purdy start to rise, and heard him answer: "How'll I know?" He looked back to the half-breed, saw the lips move, but didn't hear the answer.

"You didn't ask me that about the Injun."

"This is different. It's gotta be done, and quick. Awful quick." Purdy's voice sank again into a blur of insistent words. "Before he talks to anyone."

Russel's eyes glinted as Dexter shoved his ale mug away and turned to Berl. His voice was harshly sibilant, and very low, too low to carry beyond Purdy. "Get the money, Con." It was the first time he'd ever used Purdy's name, and there seemed to be a wry emphasis to it now. "I want him dead, too, remember." He shrugged slightly. "I'd've killed the sneaking buzzard, anyway, but your money'll make me hunt him down that much faster. Get it."

Purdy was convinced. He got up quickly, threw an unseeing glance at the two lawmen strolling toward the door, and hustled toward his office. There was a monstrous steel safe in there. It'd held his growing wealth for close to thirty years, ever since he had come to the Brazitos on a fast horse, down out of the colder climates of the high, northern territories.

Dexter went over to a buggy seat bolted against the wall, beneath the Parker House Saloon's overhang, and sat down. "That, Berl, was worth watching. Con's tied in with the 'breed some way." He fished for his tobacco sack with a frown. "You see Con's face, there, for a few seconds? He looked like he'd seen a ghost?"

Berl spat out the shredded remnants of his quid. "Yes, and I don't like seeing them two together." Berl sat down, too. "What a sneaky pair."

Dexter smoked, looking out over the sun-blasted, writhing roadway with its burden of manure and myriad flies. "Yeah, but that don't help us a damned bit. Not about the Digger, or Antrim, either."

Berl nodded. "I wouldn't put it past that 'breed. Both of the killings, for that matter."

"Except," Dexter reminded him, "that one man couldn't have done both of them."

Berl swore. "Well . . . now what?"

The sheriff smoked in silence for a few seconds, then flicked off an ash with his little finger. "I don't know," he said honestly. "I'll be darned if I do."

They both heard the louvered doors vibrate, and looked around. Owl Russel came out of the Parker House Saloon, let his savage glance rake over them, stepped down onto the duckboards, and walked to the livery barn.

Dex and Berl watched the man go. Owl Russel was a good-looking man, like a sleepy panther or a shiny rattler. The ivory-butted guns swayed suggestively at his hips. He stepped out into the glare of the roadway, and the avid daylight grabbed him for its own.

The sheriff saw Ed Smith shove off the shaded wall and follow the gunman into the barn. "Berl . . . what in Hades is that man going to ride out for in the heat of the day?"

"Beats me."

They sat in motionless silence until Owl Russel, mounted on his beautiful black horse, rode out through the barn's maw, swung north out of town, and rode slowly over the land. The sheriff got up suddenly.

"Come on. Let's see what Ed knows about him."

Berl followed.

The liveryman was thoughtful when Dexter questioned him. "Well . . . don't cotton to the man, personally, Dex."

"Yeah. I know. What'd he talk about?"

"The Hartmans. He asked if I'd ever heard of them. I told him sure. I told him about them folks getting killed some twenty years or so ago. Shot down in their yard, and how folks always figured maybe Indians did it. Then, later, how the rumors started that maybe Cliff Lewis knew something about it, since he got their land. Then . . . you'll recall, Dex . . . there was a story about them Hartmans having a big satchel of gold hid on the place somewhere, and folks said maybe Lewis killed them for it, and stole it."

Smith squinted through his thick lenses and warmed

to the topic, but Dexter Williams knew his man. He held up a hand, grinning slightly.

"You didn't tell him more'n that, did you, Ed?"

Smith looked surprised, then wagged his head frankly. "No, reckon not, Dex."

"What'd he say to all that?"

Smith shrugged. "Sort of laughed and said . . . 'You believe all that stuff, *hombre?*'"

"Where'd he ride to, Ed?"

Smith looked annoyed. "How'd I know? That man's the last feller on earth I'd ask any questions of. He got sore, too. He asked me did the Hartmans have folks hereabouts."

"Why'd he get sore?"

"Well . . . I commenced to describe them. Tamsen was quite a looker, I remember. He got sore and cussed at me, and said he didn't want no picture of them. So I told him Burt Hunt was Tamsen's brother, and he rode off 'thout so much as a thank you." It still rankled, too. Dexter saw it in the man's florid face. He turned to Berl with a shine in his eyes. His mouth was open to say something when Heber Kimball, riding by in the dust, saw him and reined over.

Dexter waited. Kimball stepped wearily down and led his animal into the barn's shade.

"Dexter, Cliff wants you at the old Hartman place. Faith rode back from there early and told the old man she'd met the *hombre* who killed Antrim camped there."

Berl snorted. "How'd she know who he was?"

"He told her."

"I'll be gosh darned!"

Dexter studied the CL's new foreman thoughtfully. "This thing's getting more botched as time goes on."

Heber looked from one to the other, shrugged, and turned back to his horse. "You coming?"

"Yeah, wait here. We'll get our horses."

Berl and Dexter Williams were side-by-side and silent as they strode up the duckboards toward their office. Dexter was almost past the Buckrum Land and Abstract Office when he happened to glance past the filthy window and saw the swarthy half-breed gunman standing in front of Burt Hunt's desk, talking to the older man. He said nothing until they were well past, then touched Berl's arm.

"You fetch the horses, Berl. I got something to do. See you at the livery barn in a few minutes."

Berl looked half surprised, nodded, and kept on walking. He didn't look back, so he didn't see Dexter duck between some buildings and head for the rear of the abstract office.

The big black horse was tied at the back of the building. Dexter smiled mirthlessly. Owl Russel had simply skirted the town and come back in behind Hunt's office, tied up, and gone in. He stood back out of sight until the gunman came out, swung up, and reined over toward the CL range for the second time. This time Sheriff Williams watched him until he was certain the man wasn't coming back, then he went into the land office and looked down at Burt Hunt.

"What'd he want, Burt?"

Fear came easily to Burt Hunt. It always had. His stomach squeezed in an extra droplet of acid and he belched behind a hasty hand and nodded at Dexter.

"He said Purdy seen me sitting with the man who licked him last night. He wanted to know who the man was. Where he could find him."

"Did you tell him?"

"How could I? I don't know where he is."

Sheriff Williams had known Burt Hunt ever since he was a boy. He'd often heard tales of the man's inherent, uncontrollable cowardice. Dexter's father had been Buckrum's first parson. He'd often said that Hunt was to be pitied, that he'd been built that way by God, like some men are, and their fear is an actual torture none could understand or explain. The sheriff pitied Hunt right then, too, because the man's terror at having talked to an obvious killer was still rampant. It showed in the bulging, irregular thumping of the pulse in the side of his neck.

"When he rode out of here, Burt, he headed west. Over toward the CL. You got any ideas why he went thataway? Something you said, maybe?"

Hunt's face was submerged in sweat. Even his large bald spot glistened in the subdued light of the room. "No. I thought he was going to hit me, Dex. He balled up a fist and cursed."

"Why?"

"He said the office smelled of terror. He said he was real susceptible to a stink like that. It was crazy talk,

Dex. He said it made him want to fight someone when he smelled fright in a man."

"Anything else?"

"A lot, but it didn't have nothing to do with the man who whipped him. Just a lot more crazy talk like that." Burt was relaxing under the sheriff's calming influence. He wagged his head curtly. "The man's dangerous as a snake, Dex. He scairt the hell out of me. He's got hell's fire in him . . . really, Dex."

Williams nodded thoughtfully, saw Berl riding back down toward the livery barn astride his own horse and leading the sheriff's. He turned toward the door, took a hold of the knob, and turned slowly.

"You want to tell me who that feller was who whipped him, Burt?"

Hunt's face barely changed expression, but Dexter sensed the almost pathetic resolve before Hunt spoke. "How can I, Dex? He was a stranger to me, too."

The sheriff regarded him stonily for a few seconds, said nothing, and left the office with pursed lips. Hunt watched him go, sighed with a sound that was almost a sob, and rummaged in his desk drawer until he found the finger-smudged bottle of rye whiskey and tilted it up.

Heber Kimball and Berl waited for the sheriff to swing up, then they rode out of the barn into the crushing heat. Dexter swore exasperatedly.

"Why do so many things have to happen when it's a hundred and twenty in the shade?"

Heber smiled ruefully, but said nothing. Berl

Clausen sucked pensively on a new quid and yanked his hat brim lower over his eyes. "The heat ain't so bad. It's the twelve-mile, round-trip ride through it that'll make widows out of wives."

Heber snorted derisively. "What in Hades d'you care? You or Dex, either. You got no wives."

"No," Berl admitted. "But supposing we ever did get spliced. What woman'd want a husband who's been shriveled into a cinder by this damned sunshine, anyway?"

Even Dexter laughed at that one. Buckrum was all but deserted as the full fury of the heat bore down upon the earth. Somewhere, east of the business section of town, the melodious clamor of someone listlessly beating an anvil floated to them. Clear of Buckrum, they swung westward and rode back over the still CL, south and west.

Riding along, the sheriff pondered Owl Russel's strange behavior. He couldn't shake the belief that the man was up to something at Con Purdy's instigation. He looped the reins, made a meticulous cigarette, offered the sack to Heber, was refused, and pocketed it. He lit up and inhaled with a mental reservation to have a talk with Purdy when they got back to Buckrum. The smell of his sweating horse came up, like old copper. The heat was murderous even at a slow gait, but in spite of its disconcerting force he thought of Bull Antrim.

Even dead, Antrim caused him discomfort. From Antrim, his mind flicked over to Cliff Lewis. He wondered why in tarnation the old rancher had kept Bull as his foreman all these years when he wasn't worth a damn for anything, unless it was bullying riders and being loud-mouthed when he was drunk. Then he thought of Faith Lewis and marveled that anything as wholesome and clean-limbed could've sprung from old Cliff. His eyes raked over the crushed land. All of it was CL. Berl's voice jerked him back to the present ride.

"This got any tie in with what we were talking about earlier?"

"Darned if I know, Berl. This much, maybe. We know Antrim's killer's hereabouts. Maybe we can get him." The lean shoulders rose and fell. "That'll be the most important thing, anyway. If we never get the Digger's killer, it won't make a lot of difference, I don't reckon."

"No," Berl said dryly. "I expect it really won't matter. Just the same, I'd like to know who killed the Injun."

Heber Kimball looked at Berl. "Talking about Porky John?"

"Yeah."

"We choused it a little in the bunkhouse. Must've been other Injuns. He had nothing a white man'd want, and no sense in risking your neck over a Digger."

"Maybe." Dexter was noncommittal. "But folks do funny things."

"Yeah," Berl spoke up, "like telling Faith he was the

hombre who killed Antrim. Now, what kind of a damned fool'd shoot his mouth off like that? And on CL range at the time?"

Heber squinted into the distance as though trying to send his eyes and ears on ahead. "I don't know, unless the feller's crazy . . . or something. Or, maybe, he just likes to brag."

Dexter said nothing. He was still examining Owl Russel's strange behavior, seeking a key to it, and finding nothing helpful at all.

Berl mopped his face with a shirt cuff. He terriered off a fresh chew of fuzz-encrusted tobacco and dropped the plug back into his shirt pocket. He felt the flow of saliva run protectively in and mix with the sweetish tang, swallowed a tiny bit tentatively, found the mixture just right, and swallowed more before he spoke again.

"I've been thinking about this other thing, Dex." He looked at Heber by way of explaining. "Dex says sometimes things happens in twos. Like Antrim and the Digger getting killed the same day. Trail of coincidence, sort of. Well . . . maybe he's right. More'n likely is. But what I say is this. It ain't so much that two men are dead, killed about the same time and day, in twos, sort of, as it is the cause of their killings. See?" He looked worriedly with a screwed-up frown on his forehead at the CL foreman. Kimball said nothing. Just looked blankly at the deputy.

Berl went on. "It couldn't have been the same killer, and yet they both got it the same day. Darned near the same hour. I'd like to know what they was killed over . . . not who done it. If I knew *what* caused them to get killed, by God, I could walk right out and put my finger on the killers, easy."

Heber Kimball flashed a wry look at Dexter, and back to Berl. "You feel all right, Berl? The sun. . . ."

"Aw . . . go suck eggs!" Berl was embarrassed. "I have an idea that if we knew how to ride this trail of twos, and figure out what caused these men to die, we could latch onto the killers 'thout moving out of Buckrum. Providing, of course," he added hastily, as he saw Kimball's critical look, "that they're still around the country somewhere."

Sheriff Williams was frowning the width of his broad forehead. "I got to sit that one out, Berl. It's too botched for me. All I know is that, if we keep poking and prying, we'll eventually find the *hombre* who shot Antrim." He shrugged. "About the Digger's killer, I wouldn't want to bet. Besides, a dead Injun's just a dead Injun, but Bull Antrim's the foreman of the CL, and there's a whale of a difference."

"*Was* the foreman," Heber corrected.

Dex nodded. "Was the foreman." He ran a long finger over the edge of his nose and whipped away a tickling streamer of sweat.

"I've got no ideas how crimes are solved. But I do know from experience that, if a lawman keeps pecking away, eventually he finds something. Perseverance, it's called."

Heber Kimball spoke garrulously. "Well, ever since

I've been with you boys, and around town, one thing's been bothering me. Just why do folks always call Bull's killer a murderer?"

The sheriff looked over at him in surprise. "Well . . . Bull was murdered, wasn't he? I mean, by God, he'd better be, because the buzzard was buried this morning."

"No, I don't mean that. Sure, he was dead all right. But who says he was murdered?"

"Well . . . wasn't he?"

"Not that I know of. It was like this. We was all taking a *siesta*. Someone came into the yard and called out . . . 'Antrim!' Bull went to the doorway of the bunkhouse, and the firing started. Bull was shot down, but when I give his gun to Berl, I looked at it. He'd fired off a shot. That makes it a fair fight, don't it? I mean, he got a crack at this stranger, so how could it be murder?"

Dexter nodded thoughtfully. "Yeah, if the gun had been fired, then I reckon he got in his licks, which sure as Hades makes it a fight instead of a murder."

Heber looked his puzzlement at the sheriff. "You got the gun, haven't you?"

Berl nodded. "Sure he has. I put the thing on his desk myself, when the coroner was through with it."

Dexter squirmed a little in the saddle. "I got it all right, but I never looked at it. Berl did."

Heber Kimball made a long face. "Fine sheriff you are," he said acidly.

Dexter looked up quickly for the grin, gesture, or

anything that would take the sting out, saw none, and was setting his teeth together when Berl spoke.

"Maybe it was like this." He knew Dexter Williams pretty well. "Sometimes a man isn't careless, or indifferent, so much as he's just darned well satisfied, inside of himself, with the way things go."

Heber regarded him woodenly. "You don't mean that Dexter's sort of glad, maybe, that Bull got it, do you?" He didn't wait for an answer. "That's all right. I make no secret that I feel the same way. That goes for the riders at the CL, too."

Dexter was still not quite over the bite of Heber's comment. He shook his head. "The law's not supposed to take sides. If Bull got killed, liking him or disliking him don't change a thing. The law's got to investigate the killing and decide whether it was a fair fight or not. That's what we've got to do now . . . investigate and decide."

Heber grunted and began to make a cigarette in the meager shade of his beaver belly Stetson. "Well . . . nobody actually saw the fight but the ones nearest to it. The boys in the CL bunkhouse sure saw and heard Bull shoot back at the stranger, and they're as close to witnesses as you can get. They'll all say it was a fair fight." He licked the paper, lipped it, lit it, and inhaled with finality. "Anyway, Antrim's been asking for it for ten years that I know of, and longer, if part of the tales about him are half true." He exhaled solemnly. "The darned wonder is that the buzzard never got it before."

Berl nodded agreement, but said nothing. He stole a look at Dexter's face. He knew the look well enough. The sheriff agreed inwardly because he was human, and therefore incapable of unbiased judgment, especially since Antrim's background around Buckrum had never been anything but bad, but he'd be flogged and dragged behind wild horses before he'd ever say so.

They had ridden a little better than half the distance to the Hartman place when Dexter threw up his arm and pointed. "Look yonder. There goes a rider. Who you reckon it is?"

Heber's eyes slitted against the glare. He saw the man a long way off, and studied him. Berl, too, stared. It was hard to see much of the man, but it wasn't hard to make out the horse. Heber shook his head, hesitated, and squinted harder, then shook it again emphatically. "I don't know who he is, but I'm sure of one thing. He's no CL rider. We don't have any grulla-colored horses in our using strings."

Berl started violently in the saddle. An oath ripped out of him.

Dex looked over in surprise. "What bit you?"

"Oh, nothing," the deputy answered sarcastically. "Nothing at all. I just put two and two together and came up with something."

Heber grinned at the sheriff. "That two stuff of his."

Dexter ignored Kimball. He knew Berl's moods too well not to be impressed with the present one. "What's up, Berl?"

"We're headed for the old Hartman place to catch a killer. We see a man loping away from us in the distance on a grulla horse. That *hombre* who whipped the 'breed two-gun man rides a grulla horse. I seen it at Ed Smith's livery barn." He waved briefly at the disappearing rider. "There goes the grulla and, more'n likely, the man we're after. He's coming from the direction of the old Hartman place, and he's not a CL rider. It all fits pretty well, don't it?"

Heber nodded, staring at the distant rider, growing smaller all the time. He looked over at Dexter, whose thoughtful expression indicated he agreed with his deputy. The CL foreman sighed. "Fine. We've ridden half across the damned country for nothing."

Williams spat cotton in disgust. "The devil with him. If he stays in the country, we'll get him. We'll ride on in and get a drink of that spring water, anyway."

The CL cowpunchers saw three riders coming over the shimmering distance and watched their approach. They were almost to the gate before Cliff Lewis looked around and let his eyes focus. Heber Kimball looked strangely at his employer, sitting out in the sun on his horse, and knew something was wrong. He nodded uncertainly, swung past Lewis, and rode on over to the CL hands. Dexter Williams and Deputy Clausen stopped beside the rancher. Their voices were lost to Heber as he swung down. The edge of the house separated the two groups. He looked at the riders and frowned.

"What happened? You *hombres* look like you been kicked in the belly?"

A heavy-set man with a spindly rear and massive shoulders below a pocked face looked up soberly. "Cliff give Faith the worst god-damned tongue-lashing I ever heard. He claimed she was disloyal and let a murderer get away. Said her streaking it over here and warning him off was the most contemptible thing he ever seen. Worse than blasphemy, he said. Even worse than murder." The man took a long drag off his cigarette. "Then she took into him. We couldn't help but hear. She near accused him of murdering these here Hartmans. It hit the old man where he lives. He jerked up real white in the face, then she turned that chestnut mare and rid back toward home."

Heber looked at the other riders. They all nodded agreement and said nothing. "Then it was Faith who let this gunman get away?" He expected no answer and got none. The men were watching him. He slumped down in the shade and made another cigarette. "Faith doing a thing like that! I can't understand it."

The cowboy nodded. "Neither," he said softly, dryly, "could the old man. If she'd been a man . . . even his own flesh . . . I believe he'd've shot her down then and there."

"Well . . . it's bad," Heber said. "But I'm beginning to wonder if there ain't something to this mess we don't know nothing about." He looked around, saw the men languishing back into their comfortable silence, and puzzled the thing over to himself. He heard the dull thunder of Cliff Lewis's voice around in front as he talked with the sheriff and his deputy.

Chapter Four
A RASH DECISION

The rancher looked at Dexter Williams disconsolately. "He's gone."

Dexter nodded his head slowly. "We figured as much, Cliff. 'Specially after we seen the grulla horse 'way off, ahead of us."

Cliff's usually calm, arrogant mask of a face was awry now. "We never saw him at all. He was gone before we got here."

"How come he left?"

Berl saw the quick agony and was surprised, until he heard the answer. "Faith rode over and warned him off. He'd left by the time we got here."

Berl scowled and said: "But why'd she warn him off after telling you what he said, and that he was here?"

Lewis's eyes raked over the deputy. This was hitting him close to home. He'd never been a man who explained things to anyone. Now, though, he did. "She said she didn't want to cause any trouble."

"Remorse, kind of," Berl said, looking at the ground and nodding. "They tell me women are like that." He suspected another reason as well, but didn't voice it. It wouldn't alter anything. The main fact was that the grulla horse and its rider were gone.

Dexter Williams got down with a grunt and headed for the spring. "I'm as dry as a bone," he said. "Be back in a minute."

Cliff Lewis dismounted then, too, and looked at the shattered sign Rezin had torn off the log wall. Without looking at Berl, he spoke absently. "Well . . . we know who killed Bull Antrim, anyway."

Berl looked at the ground for a long second, sighed, and swung down. "This here Hartman *hombre?*"

"Sure. Who else? He told Faith who he was and said he'd killed Bull. That's good enough for me and the CL."

Berl got the meaning behind the last three words. The CL was its own law and would settle its own wars. Hartman would be a target for CL guns as long as he lived, which, the way Cliff Lewis's face looked right then, wouldn't be long.

Dexter Williams's spurs rang musically as he came back from the spring. "Cliff," he said in his soft, unhurried way, "why is this Hartman *hombre* so dead set on killing folks, anyway? You know?"

Lewis shrugged. "This is the yard where his people were killed." A thick hand pointed toward some cottonwoods beyond the seepage from the box spring. "See that ground between them trees there? That's where they're buried. Right there." The arm dropped. "He's looking for the killers, I reckon. They were never caught."

Dexter raised the edge of a forefinger to the inside corner of one eye, then the other, to test for sleepy seeds, occasioned by summer eye strain. "Well," he said, "at least we know who we're looking for, although I'm not sure he's really broken any laws."

"What!"

Dex stood his ground before the wrath in Lewis's face. "Bull got off a shot, Cliff. He wasn't strictly murdered. He shot in self-defense. That makes it a killing, but not murder."

Cliff Lewis blinked woodenly at the sheriff, then his lip curled back over his teeth. "Dex, that's the kind of law that buried them Hartmans. Blind law. Indifferent law." He started toward his horse. "Well, the CL don't take to that kind of justice. No, sir! You can let it slide if you want to, but we won't. No man rides onto the CL and shoots down a man and rides away scot free." He went past the corner of the house, saw his riders and their foreman squatting in the shade, and jerked his head at them. "Come on, boys. Let's get back."

They all mounted and rode across the yard behind Lewis. He stopped near the gate and looked down at Dexter.

It was at this precise moment that a lone rider, far off over the range, sat still and slitted his black eyes through the glare toward the old house. He saw six men on horseback sitting in the yard, close to a pair of riderless but saddled horses.

"Dexter, you either find that Hartman *hombre* and jug him, or the CL'll find him. Won't no one ever see him again, or jug him either, if the CL gets to him first." Lewis swung abruptly away and rode out of the yard, followed by his riders.

Sheriff Williams's face was a deeper red under its perpetually scorched exterior as he watched the CL men ride back down the land the way they had come. He didn't speak, but Berl read his thoughts, and they weren't pleasant ones.

Cliff Lewis was big. No getting around that. And powerful. But, unless he was duly elected sheriff, he'd better not try to run the sheriff's office!

The deputy interrupted the silence. "Well . . . we got enough to corral this Hartman. Now all we need is grounds to get the 'breed, too."

Dexter still said nothing. His eyes had picked up the small speck of a lone rider in the far distance. He reckoned it to be the gunman on the grulla horse, but he was wrong. Glumly he squatted in the shade of the house and made a cigarette. The lone horseman far out over the range wasn't Rezin. It was Owl Russel searching for Rezin.

The two-gun man turned back with curses. Either Rezin Hartman had a lot of friends, or there were a lot of men who weren't his friends, looking over the old Hartman place for him. He'd had a long ride, too, for nothing. The black horse went around the upper end of Razorback. Owl figured, as long as he was out this far on CL range, he'd scout it a little ways before heading back to Buckrum. Nothing doing in town anyway, until after nightfall.

It irritated him, just the same. There was an uneasy stirring within him. Like a gigantic pair of black wings were fluttering. Ominous and unpleasant. Normally he didn't have half as much trouble getting to a victim, and he didn't like it.

Owl was riding along, brooding, when he saw the elegant mare in the near distance, approaching a rambling set of buildings he guessed must be the headquarters of the CL. He rode doggedly along, watching the oncoming rider. They'd meet just about where the trails converged on the tree-lined lane into the ranch yard proper. He felt a little exultation that was unusual, and irritably shrugged it off as the two horses saw each other and went forward with ears up, curious.

Owl was no more surprised to see Faith than she was to see the broad-shouldered, hard-faced man on the beautiful black. She blinked up at him and admitted to herself that he was handsome, in spite of the obvious marks of a recent fight.

Owl Russel's smile, so rarely used, was dazzling. It completely changed the look of his face, which, at its worst, wasn't bad-looking, with the clean-cut, almost severe features and compelling black eyes. He nodded with a slight sweep of his head that acknowledged her. He'd often thought, in rare weak moments, that if and when he ever married, it'd have to be something like this green-eyed girl on the chestnut mare.

"G'day, miss."

"Good day. Are you looking for someone? I'm Faith

Lewis. My father is Cliff Lewis. He owns this range. The CL." She looked down the lane as a shadow passed over her face. "He isn't home right now, but if you'd care to wait, ride on down the lane. He'll be along before very long."

"Don't you live here, too?"

Faith had made up her mind as she had ridden back. It was a rash and harsh decision. But she would not—could not—stay on the CL and face her father as long as she felt as she did.

"Well . . . I'm just stopping long enough to get some . . . things, then I'm going on into Buckrum and get a room at the Parker House."

Owl blinked swiftly. Instinctively he'd known the huge CL was a barrier, like a moat, that he could never cross to get to this beautiful girl. But if she lived in the Parker House, where he also had a room. . . . He smiled again. The flash of his teeth, white and even in the dark skin, was amazingly pleasant.

"I'll ride with you, if you don't mind. I've got to get back to Buckrum, too." He watched the bewilderment come into her eyes and shrugged. "I didn't particularly want to see Mister Lewis. I was just sort of riding around Buckrum to get the lay of the land."

"Oh," Faith said hesitantly. "I suppose . . . well, all right."

It didn't take her long. Mostly she took a heavy pouch of gold coins that were her savings, then went back outside. The burly Indian housekeeper watched with inscrutable eyes as Owl Russel handed her into the saddle and raked her over with his obsidian eyes as she swung up. The woman's face was impassive, but the eyes weren't.

Faith was naturally curious about the dark stranger on the handsome black horse. She surreptitiously noticed his lean, flat hips encircled by shell belts for twin guns. She knew he was no cowboy, and wondered if, maybe, he was a gunfighter. Doubts assailed her. Her feverish mind had led her into a position that made her uneasy.

"You're new to the Brazitos, aren't you? I mean . . . I've never seen you in Buckrum before."

Owl nodded. "Yes, miss. Haven't been here but a couple of days."

"Passing through?"

He was inwardly amused: *Nosy, like Liza.* The thought and comparison made him grimace slightly. "No, not exactly. I'm looking for a man." He wondered if he dared ask her, or if she'd know anything about Hartman, anyway. Her next comment turned the conversation into safer channels, though, and he let it stay there.

"You thought my father might know him?"

Owl nodded without speaking.

Faith felt relief. She was surprised, too, that she hadn't thought of it before, because the stranger obviously wasn't a cowboy. The twin guns, the magnificent horse, and his remark about looking for a man probably meant he was an undercover lawman. Then her heart skipped a beat. Perhaps he was investigating

Rezin Hartman. He might have been hired to hunt down Antrim's killer. Maybe it had been by her father! It was wholly possible. She'd met him at the entrance to the CL lane.

Unconsciously she arraigned herself on Rezin's side in the enigma and took her stand in silence as they rode over the range, eastward, toward Buckrum. The gathering storm of doubt made her put it bluntly.

"Are you a peace officer?"

"In a way," he answered, smiling inwardly again. He'd been wondering how he'd work it. She had supplied the means herself. His tongue flashed over dry lips, and the crawling under his skin was beginning, very gently, but he felt it, nevertheless.

"How'd you like to help me find this man? You know the country, miss, and I don't." He frowned slightly.

She noticed how cruel the frown made his face, and waited for him to go on.

"I'll get you the room at the Parker House and have your meals sent up. No one'll know you're there. Then we can talk. You can tell me all about the people and the country hereabouts, see? And I catch my man." He shrugged his powerful shoulders. "Otherwise, it might take me a month to find him." His coal-black eyes were expressionless and watching.

Faith made her decision in a flash. He was after Rezin, and fate had thrown her across his trail so that she could aid Hartman. She nodded quickly. "All right. I'll do it."

Languid shadows were enveloping Buckrum when Owl Russel left Faith at the back of the Parker House Hotel, went in through the kitchen, crossed the card room, and leaned over the tiny counter where the room clerk sat drowsily, looking over the smoky haze of the room, watching the players.

"That room next to mine. I want it." He put a crumpled paper bill on the counter. The clerk flashed him a sidelong glance, pursed his lips, and fished a key out of the drawer by his knees. He made rapid change, and handed it over. Owl left one of the cartwheels lying in front of the man. He looked up, startled, saw the saturnine stare, smiled, and let his shoulders rise and fall. Owl turned away.

Faith was decidedly uneasy by the time Owl guided her to the room and handed her the key. She saw a brilliance in his eyes that hadn't been there before. She put the small bundle of her clothing on the battered marble-topped dresser, beside the commode basin and pitcher. He watched her take off her hat and reach back to undo the ribbon that held her hair behind her ears. He smiled again, turned, and walked out of the room.

"I'll have supper sent up to you." He looked back from the door and watched as she shook the wealth of hair loose. His throat was fiery and dry, and the crawling under his skin was becoming insistent. "I may not be back for a while. I've got some nosing around to do."

Then he was gone, and she heard the soft music of his spurs as he descended the stairway.

The desk clerk watched Owl Russel cross the card room, push into the bedlam of the saloon proper, and become lost in the boisterous racket and mob of bodies.

The night bartender was tying his apron on and looking at the splendor of his fierce moustache in the back-bar mirror. He heard Frosty grunt softly, and let his eyes glide over the patrons reflected in the mirror until he saw the reason. The half-breed gunman had muscled in callously and was downing his sour mash like a man long without. Frosty served him two, then he flung away from the bar, ambled into the dining room on the far side of the card room, talked to a waiter, and returned to the saloon.

The night hadn't even started yet, and Owl Russel had everything running his way. Everything but Rezin Hartman. He shrugged over that, but the rancor was alive, just the same. He saw Conseil Purdy come out of his office and survey the crowd. However, there was no satisfaction on the swarthy face. Purdy had something else on his mind.

Purdy glanced along the bar until his eyes crossed with the steady malevolence of Russel's cold stare. Purdy started a little, jerked his head a tiny bit, and went over to his private table.

Owl ignored the summons, drank another whiskey mash, looked at Purdy indifferently, and watched the man suck inward on his cheek, then jab his tongue around. It was like a blind snake searching for food, feeling a ragged bit of flesh, and flash after it with his teeth. Owl felt the contempt coming up, and let it come. Purdy flashed him another long look. He shoved off the bar and stalked through the miraculous openings that appeared in the crowd of riotous, red-faced cowboys, and stood over Purdy, looking down coldly.

"Get him?"

"No. Never even seen him. Looked high and low, too."

"Listen. You've got. . . ."

"Quit worrying. I'll get him the first chance I have."

"Maybe he's already left the country."

"I don't believe it. He's looking for someone, I think." Owl watched for—and saw—the ashen pallor come up under the dark skin.

"What makes you think so?"

"Things I've heard, and figured out. Been asking questions. He won't leave the Brazitos until he's got his man . . . or until I get him."

"Well, for Lord's sake, get him, then!"

Owl shrugged slightly, started to say something, clamped his mouth shut, and turned back to the bar. The contempt was raging inside of him. Men gave way before the insistent and cold look of his jet eyes, and Frosty looked up, saw him, and raised an eyebrow. Owl nodded.

. . .

The yellow-orange patches of light outside splashed onto the dullness of dusk with a welcome, human little symbol to Dexter and Berl as they rode back into Buckrum from the north end of town. They passed, specter-like, through the gloom, listening critically to the sounds of revelry that boiled out of the Parker House Saloon, heard no undercurrents, and rode on past.

There were few people abroad, and those few were either normal, happy couples, hand in hand, or oldsters out for a stroll after the murderous heat of the day.

The lawmen swung in at the sheriff's office. Berl sighed as he dismounted and held out a hand for the sheriff's reins.

"I'll put them in the shed and fork them over some hay."

Dexter handed him the reins without comment, unlocked the door, entered, and reached for the lantern. Its rich, soft light added another block of orange to the patterns already lying on the roadway past the door.

Dexter was thoughtful. He sat down behind his desk without removing his hat, fished out Antrim's gun, thumbed open the ejection gate, and spun the cylinder until he saw a fired cartridge. He regarded the brass casing solemnly, spun the cylinder again, and tossed the heavy gun back into the drawer.

Berl came in slapping at the cloying foxtails and hay stalks.

"Dexter, why did Lewis keep Antrim on the CL?"

The sheriff shrugged. "I have no idea. The feller was no stockman. I know that. Seen him handle horses too many times to believe otherwise. Why?"

"Well, you reckon they could've been tied in some way? Like this, maybe. Supposing Bull shot them Hartmans at Cliff's orders. He'd have to keep him handy and well fed, wouldn't he?"

"I reckon. But in the first place, I just can't see Cliff Lewis murdering women. Then, too, if this Hartman *hombre* knew Cliff had been in on the killing of his folks, like he must've figured Bull was, he'd've blasted Cliff a long time ago."

"All right. Just how did he come to know Antrim had a hand in it . . . if he did know it?"

Sheriff Williams sucked his teeth thoughtfully. "I'm guessing, Berl. Strictly guessing. He'd have to have a relative or a friend, or something, here in Buckrum, who either knew the truth or suspected it."

"No, if there was anyone around here knew anything, they'd've told the whole Brazitos long ago."

Dexter squinted. "Don't you believe it. This country's full of men who're alive today just for one good reason. They know what to keep to themselves, and when to keep their damned mouths shut."

That stopped the deputy. It was a very, very true fact, and he knew it. He finished brushing off the hay and sat gingerly on his tilted chair, squirmed tentatively, felt no signs of giving, and relaxed.

"Burt Hunt knows this Hartman *hombre*, don't he?"

Dexter yawned prodigiously. "Yeah, I talked to Burt earlier. He wouldn't tell me a thing. But I'm guessing this Hartman is his nephew. Burt's sister was Tamsen Hartman, the murdered lady. These Hartmans had a little kid. I recall that, too."

"Now we're getting somewhere," Berl said. "That'd explain a lot of things."

Dex looked at the younger man owlishly. "Berl." His voice was soft. "We got nothing. Just guesses. But it all comes together pretty well when you mull it over. I don't know why Hartman and this 'breed tangled. Don't give a darn. Hartman's out to kill the men who shot his folks. Maybe Antrim was one of them. If so, like you figure, he must've gotten his facts from the local folks. That'd be Burt Hunt, in this case."

Berl nodded. "All right. Now where's the 'breed come in?"

Dexter shook his head. "I don't know. I don't know why or where he comes in, but I do know that after Hartman whipped him he's hot for his scalp. But before that, I'll be darned if I know."

"Con might know."

Dexter arose, and yawned again. "Yeah, I've been figuring I'd have a talk with Con about that." He looked over at Berl blandly. "You want to trail along or bed down?"

Berl fingered his sprouting beard stubble. "I'll trail along."

There were a lot of small, disjointed bits of information knocking around inside his head. He couldn't have slept, anyway.

The night was just beginning to settle in earnest. Before, it had been a long dusk, typical of Southwestern summer nights. They stood on the duckboards outside the sheriff's office and breathed in the pleasant smells of the cooling earth and looked out over the shadowy angles of the little cow town.

The sounds from the Parker House Saloon came stridently down the night air. Dexter Williams stepped off the sidewalk into the dusty, iron-like roadway, heading in that direction as though pulled by magnetic force. The deputy followed.

Ed Smith was just going out of the louvered doors as Dex started in. The liveryman touched Williams's arm and jerked his head. The sheriff turned sideways and followed Ed out onto the plank walk, where they walked side-by-side southward, toward Ed's home. They went a good twenty feet before the liveryman spoke.

"Dex . . . did anything happen out at the CL today?"

"Well . . . not at the CL exactly. Berl and I went out there when Cliff Lewis sent in word that he had Antrim's killer bottled up at the old Hartman place. Why?"

"I don't know." Ed was frowning at his feet. "Only that 'breed gunman . . . you know . . . the one with the ivory butts on his guns . . . big, husky feller, dark and. . . ."

"Yeah, I know who you mean. What about him?"

"He was in the saloon drinking for a while. Then he went out the back door and led two horses down to my barn. I was having my before supper beer, y'see, so I know he come out of the Parker House. Besides, I went to the doors and watched him lead those two horses down the alley, out onto the roadway, and cut across to my barn. Also seen Cleat take them from him. Then he come back to the bar."

Dexter's patience was wearing thin. "Well . . . that don't mean much, does it?"

"Dex, one of the critters was that big black of his. But the other 'n' had a CL on its left shoulder as big as you please. I'll lay you money it's Faith Lewis's chestnut mare. The one with the flaxen mane and tail." Ed had stopped walking and was half turned so he could face the lawman. "I'd know that mare anywhere."

The sheriff was frowning. He felt like he should be able to sense something, but he couldn't. "What you getting at, Ed?"

"How come that gun hawk to have the girl's horse? You know she'd never sell it. I've tried to buy it half dozen times myself. She just wouldn't peddle that mare, that's all." Ed's voice dropped. "It was saddled, too. Faith's saddle. The one with the silver name plate on the back of the cantle." He tapped the sheriff's chest. "He's went and stole that mare and saddle sure as you're a foot tall."

Dexter blinked doubtfully. He liked Ed and

respected his shrewdness where horses were concerned. But he also knew Ed Smith as an old woman with his tongue. Besides, the liveryman's tale was the nebulous sort of thing that could lead a man to make a fool of himself. Too many maybes. Maybe the girl came to Buckrum with the gunman. Poor company, but still her business. Maybe he brought the horse and saddle to town for the Lewises some way. Maybe a hundred things. Shrugging, he smiled evasively.

"I'll take a look, Ed."

Smith nodded like a conspirator. "Wish you would, Dex. G'night."

" 'Night." The sheriff watched Ed paddle on south toward home, shook his head slightly, and went back to the saloon. He jerked his head to Berl, who had remained standing there in the shadows, and they went inside.

The Parker House was crowded. Dexter and Berl took their drinks to a far corner. The sheriff told Berl about Faith Lewis's mare. He got a quizzical stare, but no comment. Berl pointed with his chin. Dexter followed the movement and saw the 'breed gunman across the room at the bar.

Owl Russel was leaning over the bar, around the far end and feeling the security of the wall against his right elbow. His thoughts were on what awaited him. It exhilarated him, and also unnerved him a little. He didn't want to scare her off. It troubled him, though, just how he could win her. They were worlds apart.

How did men, in her world, woo their women? It rankled and angered him that, in spite of the brutal and abrupt emergence he'd made out of the sink hole he'd been raised in into this world of money and respect where he was now, there still existed a barrier.

The worst part about it, too, was that he didn't know just how to get over or around it. Not with force, he knew that. But how?

"Frosty!"

The bartender had been watching him out of the corner of his eye. He brought the drink right over. He had come to know this man's liquor needs pretty well. He had been thinking, too.

"How'd you like a bottle of sour mash I've been experimenting with . . . to take with you?"

Owl looked at him without blinking. "I'm not going anywhere."

Frosty frowned slightly. "I don't mean that. Look, just for the hell of it, I've been experimenting today with an idea of mine. I make up fifths of mixed drinks and put them already mixed into bottles, see?" He looked down into the jet pits behind Russel's eyes and saw the naked, flickering fires there.

Owl turned the idea over in his mind dully, then a shaft of light warmed him suddenly. That was it! He'd take the bottle up to her room. How simple. How ridiculously, childishly simple. He flashed a smile that startled Frosty all the way down to his stomach, because it made the man from hell's face absolutely handsome. Owl reached in a pocket, fished out several twenty-dollar gold pieces, and carefully reached far over and put them in Frosty's pale, damp palm.

"I guessed you wrong, Frosty."

The bartender turned quickly away and, with a puzzled look on his face, got the bottle from a private niche, and handed it to the 'breed gunman.

Purdy sat sipping his ale, and nodded to the sallow man at the piano. The music had a hard time of it. The place was packed with riders whose simple exuberance was maddeningly loud. Still, the man banged away, and gradually the sound carried to ears that knew what it presaged. The noise slacked off a bit, then began a gradual simmering down as word was passed.

Owl still held his bottle in one hand, and let the other hand rest around the moist little body of his empty mash glass. He knew what was coming, too, and it mixed him up inside. Liza was his type. No doubt about it, but a man who'd been so merciless in bringing himself up this far shouldn't settle for a Liza Bent. Or should he? Maybe she'd always understand and tolerate where the other—the green-eyed one— wouldn't. He swore viciously to himself and forced the caroming thoughts out of his head.

Absently Owl noticed the sheriff and his deputy across the room. They were watching him, stony-faced and motionless. He curled a lip and looked away. The devil with them, too. He looked back at the card room door, watching for Liza, and a crazy thought occurred to him that Faith Lewis was going to come strolling in, in that dress of Liza's, and sing to him. He flagged Frosty for another whiskey mash, numbly clutching the full bottle.

Dexter was still nursing his ale. He spoke to Berl without taking his eyes off the dark gunman. "Getting drunker'n a Siwash, Berl. Be trouble now, sure."

"How about Faith's mare?"

"The devil with the thing. The man's here. We want an excuse to nail him, not the horse."

Berl drained his glass. "Seems to me we ought to be hunting the other one. Hartman. We got reason to corral him."

Dexter was nettled. "Sure, but we can't be in two places at once. Besides, we got to wait for him to show up again."

"Maybe he's sloped."

"No, he's got one of them. There's sure to be more."

"Why?"

"Because he's still in the Brazitos, two days after killing Antrim. We know that from Faith's old man."

Berl nodded. "Makes sense," he said, "but I'd like to know where he's hid out, just the same."

Berl would have gasped if he could have seen Rezin, right then. He was lolling back on his blankets by the box spring, watching the night descend and wondering just how a girl like Faith Lewis would go about finding out what hadn't been found out in twenty years.

Rezin had made a large circle after he had left Faith,

and waited along the craggy, reflecting sides of Razorback until the riders had all left. Then he had clambered onto the volcanic pile and surveyed the country, and seen a man on a black horse and what appeared to be a smaller man on a chestnut, riding toward Buckrum. Then he'd come down, waited for dusk, and ridden back to the old ranch and bedded down.

In a way he hated himself for letting the Lewis girl's pleadings make him wait, because it had cost him the element of surprise that he had meant to use against her father. But, on the other hand, maybe she could find out something, and it was important that he knew, for certain. He didn't want to kill an innocent man— or men.

He lay back, not thirty feet from the graves he didn't know were there, and smoked lazily, watching the high sky and letting his thoughts drift back to that strange, half-savage kiss.

Again Owl compared Faith Lewis with the tawny singer at the Parker House. Again he made a wry face at the comparison. He remembered the way Liza sang, like she was singing at this moment, in the smoke-murky saloon. She sang one song, and Owl's eyes never left her. She had seen him and looked away. He didn't move as she threw that half-disdainful glance at the cowboys, and started through the card room door. She hesitated only long enough for Purdy to stop chewing his cheek and toss a handful of coins at her to start the avalanche, then came back into the room with that rolling-hipped walk that made the men shout and stamp their feet.

Owl didn't appreciate the act. He'd seen it the night before. His eyes were baleful and brooding. He let his thoughts cruise unchecked.

She was looking straight at Owl Russel when she sang the second song. Dimly, through the hum inside his head, he recognized the melody and the words. He also recalled telling her, last night, that he liked the way she'd sung that song, "Gary Owen". Some of the red film cleared away. He knew she'd forgiven him, then, and a shaft of gallantry, ragged and weak, raised itself—barely—inside of him. He appreciated her forgiveness, and started through the crowd even before her song had ended.

The men who had seen her after she had gone out with Owl Russel the night before watched. Their judgment would be based on how she acted now. If she froze him in his tracks, he might kill all of them, but they'd uphold her honor. If she went with him, they'd brand her forever with a name, and Owl Russel could kill her; they wouldn't turn from their drinks to watch.

Liza knew this, by feminine instinct, and Owl did, too, although how he knew it he didn't know himself. Liza's song ended. She looked into Owl's face. The tension was thick.

He didn't smile, just jerked his head curtly toward the table they had started from the night before, barged on past, ignoring her—and she followed. The men at the bar saw and condemned, and looked away in contempt. Liza felt it and let her savagery flaunt it.

"It was the liquor." She swam a little in his vision.

"Ruint the dress."

Owl fished out two limp paper one hundred dollar bills and shoved them across the table at her. She crumpled them and shoved them into the front of her dress as Owl caught Frosty's glance.

The barman was done for the day, taking off his apron when the silent summons came. He did an about-face, made up the drinks, and took them over. He owed the 'breed that much, anyway, for the gold pieces.

Owl shoved the watered whiskey across. "Satisfied now, Liza?"

"I reckon, Owl." She swished the liquor around inside the glass. "What's wrong with you?"

"Me?" It startled him. "Nothing. Not a thing. Why?"

She shrugged.

Owl swore under his breath. She was his type. Maybe, later, the nagging in his guts would let him think more clearly than he could right now. Then he'd figure how to win the green-eyed one, and maybe marry her. He had forgotten the purpose of his generosity with Frosty, who he saw leaving the saloon by the louvered doors, after throwing them a significant look.

Swiftly Owl reached out and caught a cowboy by the shirt and pulled the surprised man in close, holding up the bottle. "Here, pardner, keep this for me. I don't want it right now. Take a little if you want, but save some for me." He looked into the flushed, puzzled face, nodded curtly, and pushed the man away.

The cowboy went over by two others, spoke in a low voice, and showed them the bottle. They cast quick looks at Owl, who was having trouble getting out of the booth. They snickered at one another, looked over at the doors, then back to one another again, and laughed out loud.

Liza saw the three of them strolling by with exaggerated slowness as Owl touched her shoulder and jerked his head toward the stairs. She got up and led the way. She knew a hundred eyes, at least, were following her and the brawny breadth of Owl's shoulders, and flung an imaginary phlegm of contempt down at them. She'd give in, readily enough, but it had to be a man, a real man.

Owl stood on the landing after climbing the stairs. The sweat was running down under his ribs from exertion. He saw Liza turn abruptly in the middle of the hallway. His eyes took in the somber shadows indifferently that normally he'd have been wary of.

"Owl?"

He grunted, knowing vaguely the men down below could see them plainly enough, despite the dinginess of the light on the landing.

"You look sick."

It angered him, and he swore viciously. Partly because he hadn't expected her to say anything like that, and partly, too, because he felt sick and hated it, associating sickness of any kind with weakness.

"Am not."

She was regarding him unblinkingly, sure of her ground this time. "You're pretty drunk, Owl."

"Like hell." Something unpleasant, like a warning, tiptoed across his consciousness. He'd been pretty drunk the night before. That's how he had been beaten by Hartman. Well, he'd learned his lesson. For twenty years he'd guarded against that situation. Yet he'd finally succumbed to it and been caught just like he had always known it would happen, if he got too drunk. It made him uneasy. It could mean that he was slipping finally. That the precise machine that he had forced himself to become was breaking down. The thought angered him. He swore again and clenched his fists. He was sweating like a spent horse. The fumes in his head merged with the sense of illness. It made his legs feel like water. He lowered his head and shook it, then looked over at her again. The silence grew between them while she studied him. His breathing was easier now, so he moved forward, deeper into the shadow and away from the blank looks from below the bar.

The noise downstairs was miles away. He didn't know that it had slackened as five hard-eyed riders, with cocked carbines in their hands, were standing spraddle-legged behind a wild-eyed, mahogany-skinned old man whose face was set in rigid lines of violence.

Owl's strength partially returned. He smiled at Liza. She returned the smile very slowly, mirroring her knowledge of holding him in her hand now. She knew the liquor fumes were dying out in his head by the loss of that awry look in his eyes.

Conseil Purdy had seen Liza and the gunman on the landing. He had mixed feelings about it, but didn't have time to make any decisions—which he wouldn't have made, anyway—before Cliff Lewis was framed in his saloon doorway with the rabid sheen of death stained into his face like acid. Purdy was shaking in spite of himself. He fought for control in the moment that it took for the saloon to smell death, with its frontier sixth sense, turn, and see it in the doorway.

By the time Cliff was in the room, and his CL cowboys with their carbines were ranging out behind him, staring into the crowd, Purdy had come to life. Gripping his cheek lining between his teeth, he forced himself off the bench and forward on legs that doled out the steps as though each might be his last. Cliff saw him coming, and let his wild eyes wash over the soft body behind its good cloth. They watched the nugget on the watch chain wave gently with Purdy's stride, then flashed back upwards.

"Where's a 'breed gunman who rides a black horse and wears two guns with ivory butts?"

Purdy felt like someone had hit him in the stomach with a lead boot. "Don't know, Cliff. I. . . ."

"Don't Cliff me, you greasy whelp!"

Purdy spread deprecating hands outward, palms down. "Don't make no trouble in here, Mister Lewis."

Out of the corners of his eyes he saw the young deputy coming out of the card room. He saw the man stop, stare, then walk forward purposefully. He let a ragged little sigh out of his throat, but strangled it at the lip level. The deputy went by him, eyes tawny and fearless.

"What's the trouble, Cliff?"

Lewis eyed Berl angrily. "Where's Dex?"

"In the card room. I'll get him if you. . . ."

"No. I don't want him. I want a black-hided skunk with two ivory-butted guns who rode off with my daughter. Keep Dex out of this, Berl. I'm going to kill me a 'breed."

Berl was aghast. His mind was racing. He recalled—too late—what Ed Smith had said. He thought of Dex and wished with all his soul that the sheriff would walk into the saloon right then. Lewis was eyeing him savagely. Berl turned abruptly. He had to get Dexter. There were five carbines and death in the doorway of the Parker House Saloon.

Berl felt like he was walking on stumps as he crossed the saloon heading for the card room. The place was deathly still. An aura of shock seemed to hold everything—and everyone—immobile. Even the suspended flight of the stuffed eagle over the back bar seemed leaden with a stiff inability to look normal.

Cliff Lewis watched Berl go. For a moment he remained still, then he swung around, shouldered through his riders, and growled an order. They followed him out.

∙ ∙ ∙

It was a warm, sultry night, the kind that acts restlessly on men, makes them uneasy. Owl Russel had cause to be unnatural. Perhaps the nearing finale of violence that drove him was transformed, some way, to his deadliest enemy, for Rezin Hartman, also, was restless, far out over the still CL land, on his pallet.

But it was Conseil Purdy, of them all, who acted. As soon as the last CL rider had disappeared beyond the slatted doors, he spun around and darted up the stairs and faced Owl and Liza, casting one twisted look over his shoulder to see if the CL had returned.

Owl was sobering a little. He stood near Liza, talking earnestly. He saw Purdy, and checked an impulse to swear at him when he saw the look on the man's face.

"Owl! Beat it! Get out of here. The whole CL outfit's looking for you. Lewis himself was in here with enough guns to fight a war." His eyes went beyond the gunman to Liza. "Get him out quick!" He pointed to a window. "Go out that way. You can't make it through the saloon."

Owl turned back toward the girl without changing facial expression. She was watching him, large-eyed and frightened. He whirled away, shoved out through a dingy window at the end of the hallway, and let himself drop about six feet to the roof of an adjoining building.

The restlessness of the murky, cloying night made him want to curse, to revile Lewis and everyone else.

He looked over the land beyond Buckrum from his rooftop vantage point, and wished he was far out over the dead expanse of empire that belonged to the man who was hunting him down.

There was another man just as uneasy, where Owl Russel wished he was. It was Rezin. He smoked and thought, and tried to relax. Nothing helped. He finally got up, pulled his boots back on, thoughtfully shucked the extra weight of his spurs, and began to walk through the darkness. The night wasn't half over. The wait would be long and dreary.

He went through the gate hole and crossed the vague trail, and headed aimlessly over the range. Maybe walking would ease the strange, unreasonable tension inside of him. He made another cigarette and smoked that as he walked. He was convinced now that he never should have put his trust in Faith Lewis. She was a lovely thing, though. He swore. Her beauty had nothing to do with it!

In the long years of planning and practicing for his deadly revenge, he had never once dreamed of a girl entering into the affair at all. But now there was one. And suppose, after thinking it all over, she decided against him and told her father he would be at the ranch at dawn? He swore again, more vigorously, and squatted on the warm earth in the dry and brittle grass. A man could be more kinds of a fool than any other animal! It was truer than he knew.

Chapter Five
REVELATIONS

Cliff's eyes raked over the stalled chestnut mare, batting her eyes sleepily at the lantern held up by Cleat. The hostler smelled more strongly than ever of slops, and he was shaking with fear.

Lewis turned, with a dry sniffing, toward him. "Who brought this mare in, boy, and how long ago?"

" 'Breed feller brought her in. He led his own horse, a big black, and this one. He come in afoot, like maybe they'd been tied close by."

"When?" It was Heber Kimball, with a harsh set to his normally pleasant features.

" 'Bout sundown, or a little after, I reckon." Cleat's arm was aching from holding the lantern up. He let it down tentatively, got no snarl, and let it hang by his knee, where he could feel the warmth through his ragged pants. Owlishly he looked at the faces surrounding him, outlined and limned by the low-hanging lantern. They were vicious and deadly faces, with the imprint of the devil's grip ingrained in each line. He shuddered in spite of himself. He was a man who had never been able to face violence and had found one escape from it in a long lifetime—bottled escape.

Heber Kimball looked at the big black horse in the number five stall. "This here the 'breed's horse?"

Cleat nodded in silence.

Heber had a weakness. It was good horses. The big

black was one of the finest he had ever seen. His eyes glowed in the semidarkness.

Cliff Lewis turned as footsteps sounded in the upper alleyway of the barn. He watched the lean, tall figure coming toward them like a silhouette animated by a purpose before he recognized Dexter Williams. He didn't speak as the sheriff came up. Their eyes locked. Lewis had never seen Dexter look so cold and belligerent as he did right then.

"'Evening, Cliff."

The rancher nodded brusquely.

"Got word you were in town loaded for bear. What's it about?"

"'Breed that's been hanging around town rode off with Faith. I'm gunning for him. You seen him?"

Dexter ignored the question, let his brittle stare wander over the CL men, all carrying their carbines, and stopped at Heber Kimball.

"Heber, is it the same 'breed that young Hartman shellacked last night in the Parker House?"

"Yeah, must be. Cliff's Injun housekeeper described him to a T. She watched him ride off with Faith, like maybe they'd met on purpose. Like it was all planned, she said."

"I don't believe that," Cliff said evenly. "Faith don't know this *hombre*. She just met him and rode off with him."

Dexter's head was wagging. "Don't make sense that way, Cliff. Why would a girl like Faith just up and ride off with the first rider she meets?"

"That's none of your business, Dexter."

Sheriff Williams's usually thoughtful, placid look hardened into something else. That was the second time the same day the same insult had been thrown at him, and he didn't like it. He stood, straight and tall, on an even eye level with the burly rancher. His voice cut the stillness like a dagger.

"Hold on a minute, Lewis. You're making trouble in Buckrum, and any trouble here is my business. Don't you ever forget it. You make a fast play here with these boys of yours and I'll blow your darned guts out past your backbone." He stopped there and let it hang like a club in the air over the bunched-up CL men and his deputy. "Now if you'll give me one good reason why Faith didn't ride off willingly with this gunman, I'll side with you in hunting her. Otherwise, you'll mount up and get out of town until you've cooled off, or I'll get me a posse and lock up the whole bunch of you, if I have to kill every one of you to do it."

Cliff's eyes were cesspools of death, writhing and contorting in the man's struggle to control himself. "Faith was leaving the CL. Why she was doing it is between her and me. She got some clothes and her money poke, and rode away. I've got it figured she planned on holing up in Buckrum for a while." A little of the man's inherent honesty came through. "I don't blame her, in a way. Everyone's got to make their own decisions." His voice rose again. "But she didn't know this 'breed . . . she couldn't have . . . and I'm positive he strung her along to get her to go with him. I want to find her, and right now! Then the CL'll show you how to make laws, right on the spot!"

Dexter's wrath had subsided. It still bubbled, but he let the last remark go by. He'd wait—then, when the time was ripe, he'd call the swaggering CL once and for all. He looked around at Berl.

"Go up to the office and fetch back two riot guns, will you, Berl?"

He watched the deputy break away and go quickly through the weak light, then he faced Heber Kimball. "Heber, you have those riders of yours put up them carbines. There's a town ordinance against packing rifles in town. But even if there wasn't, you couldn't walk around here, not while I'm sheriff, anyway, toting those things."

Heber looked at Cliff, who was glaring at Dexter.

The sheriff intercepted the look and nodded gently. "I mean it, Cliff."

Lewis swung reddened eyes toward his foreman and nodded. Heber turned to the cowboys, motioning with his head toward the livery barn tack room. They walked away without a word.

Dexter relaxed. He had usurped the command from the irate CL, and that's what he had intended to do in the first place.

While he waited for Berl to get back with the riot guns, he rolled a cigarette with slightly shaking hands and questioned Cliff Lewis. Like he'd suspected, it all centered around the 'breed gunman he and Berl had watched go up the stairs with Liza. He knew his name, too. Frosty had gotten it from Purdy. Owl Russel.

While Dexter was thinking about him, Owl lay prone and watched the CL men disappear into the black maw of the livery barn. He wanted to roar out defiance from his roof top bastion, but, also, he felt like hunkering down somewhere and sobbing like a child.

He did neither. He waited until the men were far down inside the livery barn, then he darted to the edge of the roof, dropped down, and trotted to the kitchen door of the Parker House, shoved wildly inside, got startled looks, hastened on into the small lobby, ignored the bug-eyed clerk, and swung up the stairs two at a time.

His hands were still shaking when he knuckled Faith's door. There was no sound. He knuckled again, more insistently, reached down, grasped the knob, and lunged wildly into the panel. It broke with a ripping sound and let him into the gloomy room like a plummet. He stared stupidly at the untouched bed, turned quickly, saw the bundle of clothing was gone, too, ripped out a savage curse, and ran out of the room and down the stairs, back through the kitchen and outside again. He'd intended using the green-eyed girl for his guarantee to safety. Now she was gone.

Owl heard someone running on the duckboards around in front of the hotel—Berl, after the riot guns. He crouched a little and ran down the alley blindly, glaring into the weak light, looking for a horse. He didn't dare go around in front of the saloon and steal one of them from the loaded hitch rails.

A traveler riding a rangy roan stallion had tied the animal to a stud ring imbedded in an old oak tree, on the northern edge of town away from other horses. Owl Russel made a small, triumphant sound when he saw the animal, and scuttled up to it, untied the reins, and flung up, spinning away. He let the powerful beast out in a lunging run, and lost himself in the night. The warm air whipped past his face, and sanity returned—and with it the nagging, crawling insistence inside his skin, like a million ants were walking.

Owl rocketed through the night with a fixed smile on his face. He'd ride to that old, abandoned ranch called the Hartman place. It wasn't safe during the day, but he'd spend the rest of the night there deciding what to do, then he'd ride by dawn. He cursed himself for not knowing the Brazitos better.

He wondered, too, what had frightened the green-eyed girl away, and, even while Owl was wondering where she was, Faith crossed out of the alley when she saw the clump of men, led by Dexter Williams, leave the livery barn. They looked familiar, even in the bad light, but they were clumping toward the saloon, and she ran quickly across the roadway and into the barn, forgetting them.

Cleat had just hung the lantern back on its nail— which was fortunate—when Faith dashed up to him. He started violently and let his weak mouth drop open at sight of her. She motioned imperiously toward the tack room.

"Get my saddle. The one with the silver name plate on the cantle. Hurry!"

Cleat hurried, petrified and frightened half out of his wits. He nevertheless did what he was told to do. When he emerged under the load of tangled gear, Faith had her mare up by the office door. She saddled in a flurry of excitement, sprang up, and rode out of the barn in a plunging run, turned northward, and headed out over the CL like an apparition.

Cleat watched her go in speechless dread, shaking badly. He scuttled far down into the barn, where he had some saloon slops hidden under some torn blankets, and mixed a vile blending of all the half-emptied drinks and bottles.

Dexter Williams regarded Con Purdy soberly. The lie had come out, and the sheriff knew that Purdy had sealed his own death warrant by telling it. He turned away, toward the stairs. Purdy watched him go, and felt his nerves grating. Heber Kimball remained behind a second. The foreman's words were a whisper, so that none save Conseil Purdy heard them, but they ate into his brain tissue like acid.

"I'm going to kill you for that Purdy. I'm going to come back later and kill you. I give you my word for it."

Then Heber crossed to the stairs and went up behind the others. He was close to the door when Dexter knuckled it, and Liza Bent faced them. The rampant emotions she had undergone had left her half listless and with unmistakable lines under the large, liquid eyes. She stared dully, hopelessly, at the mob of men looking at her with very still and sober eyes.

Dexter inclined his head a little. "Where is he?"

"Gone." She motioned toward the hall window.

A rider came up the stairs two at a time. Cliff looked at him.

"Find her?"

"No, the clerk said he never seen her leave, but she's not in the room."

Dexter digested it. "They didn't leave together, then. Not if he jumped out this window."

"It's possible," Berl said.

Dexter wagged his head. "I don't believe it. Not when he's running for his life. Not unless she knew he was running and meant to go with him." He nodded at the deputy. "Go down to the barn, Berl, and watch the place. He's gone, but there's always the chance he'll come back for his horse."

Berl turned without a word and stalked down the stairs, past the stares and muttered, low talk of the patrons, and outside. He was beginning to feel the sapping weariness of all this excitement.

Cliff Lewis's wildness was only half burned out. It was like old ashes in his mouth as time went by. He walked uncertainly down the stairs and looked over the balustrade at the upturned, solemn faces down in the barroom.

Dexter looked for a long moment at Liza, shrugged, and turned away. She closed the door after the last of them. Dexter noticed that Purdy wasn't at his table, probably locked up in the mole hole of an office with its big safe. He caught up with Cliff Lewis just as Berl bounded back into the room, blinked at Dexter, and spoke.

"Her sorrel's gone, Dex."

Dexter felt his wits running, like water, downhill. He was bone-tired, and showed it. "How about his black?"

"Still there. That old rummy hostler of Smith's said Faith come in no more'n ten minutes after we left, took her horse, and rid out like lightning."

Dexter was dumbfounded. "Which way did she go?"

"He says toward the CL."

Cliff's eyes lightened then. There was hope in them as he turned to his riders. "Come on, boys. She's gone back home."

They followed him outside. Only one hung back. Heber Kimball looked furtively at Conseil Purdy's office door. There was no mistaking the look. Dexter saw it, too.

"Heber, take those carbines out of Smith's office when you go. Don't come back to Buckrum with them. Pass that along to Cliff, will you?"

Heber nodded curtly, and left the saloon. No one spoke for a long time after the CL men had left. Then the low hum arose to a loud buzz, and men converged on Dexter and Berl. The sheriff pushed past them, shaking his head.

"Later, boys. Come on, Berl. It ain't over with yet, or I miss my guess."

Together they walked up the plank walk until they were across from the office. They stepped down into the cooling dust and trudged over. There was a faint smell of dawn in the air. Dexter nudged past the office door and sought his chair, after lighting the lantern. He regarded Berl with a wry smile.

"Well . . . Deputy . . . you ready to drop?"

"Darned near. Why?"

"I got an idea. Think I'll ride out over the CL."

Berl sighed. He knew perfectly well that Dexter was right. The mess, or whatever it might be, was obviously swinging into a lurid and rapid showdown of some kind. He could sense it.

"Me, too, Dex. Where we going?"

"Well . . . I don't rightly know. First off, I reckon we'll hit for the old Hartman place. Might be something brewing out there. Then maybe we'll ride over to. . . ."

"Save it. I'll get the horses saddled. We'll have plenty of time for palavering."

He turned abruptly and went out into the night. Sheriff Williams watched him go with a wry shake of his head. He admired guts any place, any time, in anyone. Berl had them.

He methodically ran a hand along the loops in his shell belt and thought of Owl Russel. A man that'd steal a woman, or whatever he had planned to do, was low enough to do anything. He thought of Rezin

Hartman, too. If he'd killed Bull Antrim—well, he shouldn't have—but maybe, when they talked to him, he'd convince them it was self-defense. Dexter thought of the blue-eyed gunman and wondered where he was, as he leaned over and blew down the lamp chimney.

Rezin was safe enough. He had felt restless, like there was something definitely bad soaking through the velvety blackness, ominous, sinister, and evil. He had caught the grulla ridgling, removed the hobbles, and saddled him. He intended to scout the CL headquarters, then skirt the fringe of Buckrum. It was a long ride with no reason, but the restlessness was rolling over him in waves now, and any action was preferable to none.

The grulla ambled comfortably through the coolness of the late night, blissfully unaware of the seared look of his rider's face. He responded to the slight pressure of the reins and swung around the upper edge of Razorback, and followed the cinder cone's slight undulation for a while, then found soft footing in the cured grass of the range proper as he walked on toward CL headquarters. Rezin's impatience made him lean forward a little in the saddle. It was in that position that he heard the loping horse coming down the night.

He reined up quickly, listened until he had placed the direction of the hoof thunder, then eased his guns in and out of their holsters. Someone was coming, and coming fast. He'd find out who he was and what he knew. If it was a CL rider, so much the better. He'd disarm him and send him on to pass the word that Rezin Hartman was still loose on the CL range.

Rezin could barely make out the rider coming toward him. He could tell the horse had come a long way, the way its hoofs hit the ground with a dragging sound. He sat perfectly still until the rider wasn't more than a hundred feet abreast of him, northward, then he leaned forward. The grulla knew what was coming and bunched his muscles for the leap that would send him careening in pursuit.

Rezin let the rider pass him a little, then he swung the big ridgling and jumped him out with a slight touch of the spurs. Dry grass and dirt flew as the horse's shoes bit in, held, and shot him forward. The first burst of speed covered more than half the intervening distance. He was almost up to the rider before he saw a fear-pinched face swing white in the moonlight toward him, the green eyes wide in terror and the cupid's bow mouth slack from surprise.

He recognized Faith as he flashed in low, reached forward, and yanked back on her rein chains. The horses slowed to an abrupt, jolting stop. Rezin straightened in the saddle with a small frown.

"You coming from Buckrum? From the sheriff's office?"

Faith had to swallow twice before she could speak. Her heart was pounding like it would tear itself loose. "Oh! You scared me half to death."

"Conscience, Miss Lewis?"

A quick, all-pervading anger replaced the chilling fear. Her eyes snapped at him. "You . . . you . . . darned fool!"

Rezin was shocked. He looked at her in perfect surprise. "What?" he said, only half willing to believe his ears.

"Charging out at me like that . . . that . . . gunfighter."

"What gunfighter?"

"The one with the two bone-handled pistols, or whatever they are. I met him this afternoon riding our range. I rode into Buckrum with him. He said, or rather I thought, he was some kind of a special lawman. He told me he was looking for a man."

Rezin nodded caustically. He knew the man, and he guessed who he had been looking for. Rezin Hartman, more than likely. "Well . . . if you liked his company so well, how come you're back?"

"There's an old man in Purdy's hotel who runs the room end of things. He told a bartender named Frosty who this man . . . his name's Owl Russel . . . had brought to the hotel. This bartender told me who Russel was . . . and what he was. I left. When you rushed out at me like that, I thought . . . naturally . . . he'd followed me."

"Where are you going now?"

Faith looked at him for a second before answering. Since there was only one home southward for close to thirty miles, and all of it CL range, she could only be going one place. There was a cutting answer all framed, but she let it die stillborn.

"I'm going home. I shouldn't have run away in the first place. I should have asked Dad . . . my father . . . right out." Her shoulders rose and fell. "I was too upset to think straight. These last few hours . . . well, they've been hell."

Rezin nodded. He could understand that. Only for him it had been these last few years. "Come on. I'll ride with you."

He waited for her to ease the chestnut mare forward. They rode stirrup to stirrup. Neither said anything for a long time, then Rezin spoke again.

"I think it's foolish for me to let you try and run this thing down for me. You've had half a day and a night, and haven't found out anything yet . . . have you?"

She looked over at his profile in the moonlight, and reined up her mare. He stopped, too, and looked over at her. There was a testy flash to her glance, but it was too dark for Rezin to see it.

"Listen, Mister Hartman, you gave me until dawn. Is your word good, or isn't it?" She waved disdainfully toward his gun belt and its lethal cargo. "Maybe you're another gunfighter, another natural killer who doesn't make his word good. If that's it, then forget I even offered to help you. If not, wait until dawn before you say I've failed."

For some reason her logic, as well as her manner, tickled him. He smiled, chuckled, then laughed outright, throwing back his head. She watched, stung, shook out her reins, and rode on at a walk, straight-backed and stiff in the saddle. Rezin eased forward and let the grulla catch up.

"Faith . . . Miss Lewis. Wait a second. I'm a little sour, maybe, but ye gods, lady, I haven't earned that tirade yet."

"Well. . . ." It was doubtful and defensive.

He laughed again. Softly this time. "Well, nothing. You have until dawn, like I said, but. . . ."

"No buts."

"All right. No buts." He stopped there, still slightly amused, and looked over at her. He could feel an odd humor emanating from her. Rezin Hartman had never seen hysteria in his life, so when he laughed over at her and she laughed back, the sound getting more shrill and abandoned with each second, he was appreciative, at first, then gradually amazed and appalled.

Faith's nerves were crawling like little snakes of ice inside of her. They tickled and hurt at the same time. She writhed against them and didn't hear the sound of her own wild, crazy laughter. She knew her mare had stopped, and she heard someone's spurs jangle as boots hit the ground. Then talons grasped her shoulders and pulled at her. She fought like a tiger, with the vision of a dark face and brilliantly cold eyes staring into her. The talons tightened and yanked. She lost her balance and fell into his arms and gave up. The fight had been useless. He had her finally, anyway. The laughter was great, racking sobs that half convulsed her. She was forced upright and held taut against a bone-hard body and, strangely, the cruel black eyes disappeared.

Someone was stroking her head and patting her awkwardly on the back. The sobs died, a little at a time, until she lay against Rezin, exhausted. He reached around, tilted her head back, and looked down into the green eyes swimming in tears.

"Easy, honey. Easy." He held her off a little and let her down onto the ground gently. She could make out his features in a shimmer of wetness. He sank down next to her, looking more dumbfounded than solicitous. "Relax, Faith. Phew! You scared the . . . devil . . . out of me. I thought you'd gone . . . uh. . . ."

"Crazy?" It came out with the last shaken breath, and she subsided with her embarrassment and small amusement at his strained look.

"I reckon. Crazy would be a mild name for it." He plucked unconsciously at the grass. "Nerves, miss?"

"Yes," she mocked him. "Nerves, miss." She blinked away the excess moisture, sniffled, and let one last bad quiver shake her from head to heel. She looked around, found her hat, and put it on, still looking at him unblinkingly, and half smiled. "Why don't you make up your mind?"

"Huh? What about? What do you . . . ?"

"One time it's Miss Lewis. The next time it's Faith, and sometimes it's plain honey. Why don't you stick to one or the other?"

Rezin was jarred right down to his booted feet. He looked over at her, red-faced. A delicious memory of their kiss returned suddenly. He felt like he'd just stolen something very valuable and was being accused of it by the owner. His eyes dropped, and he thanked heaven for the semidarkness that hid the dark blood in his face.

"Well?"

Rezin looked up. The green eyes were ringed with bluish stains of fatigue and strain. He could see it by leaning closer. She didn't move. "Well," he said softly. "If you're going to run, or hide . . . you'd better get going."

"Hide . . . nothing!" she said, awed by her own boldness, and waiting, even anticipating a little by leaning forward just a bit.

Rezin's mouth, with its little parched cracks, brushed over her lips, came back, slowed, and rested there. He could feel the quiver in her mouth, the coolness and moistness. It was something to cherish. He savored it gently, rapturously and reverently. The kiss made a small, intimate sound in the great vault of heaven. They reared back a little and regarded each other somberly, like two strange puppies.

"Well," he said softly, "well?"

Faith sucked in a great lungful of fresh night air and shivered slightly. "Rezin."

"Yes?"

"Did you mean that?"

"Yes, that one and the other one, but I shouldn't."

"Why?"

"Because I've got doubts about your dad, and Faith,

honey, I don't want you across the fence from me. I don't want to hurt you, either. That's why."

She looked at him wistfully. "You're on a hate trail?"

"Yes."

"Couldn't you . . . isn't there something else you'd rather . . . ?"

"Faith, those were my parents. Shot down in cold blood. My father and mother. No one ever paid for their murder. I certainly owe them that."

She nodded slightly, and let her head drop a little. Something was making her age, like it had her father. She remembered something her mother had told her once, ten years ago, before she had died, something about the sins of the father being visited unto the children.

She thought of the way Cliff Lewis had looked so old all of a sudden, when she had tongue-lashed him—practically called him a murderer that morning, when he'd reviled her for warning Rezin off. She understood, too, that his sin, or at least his implication, was what had aged him—and her as well—in the last twenty-four hours.

Being twenty-one at that moment, Faith felt old and wise, and very, very sad, because she, too, suspected her father. With a doleful shove she got up and watched Rezin uncoil off the ground and face her. There was an obstacle between them, all right. She turned back, automatically felt the mare's cinch, found it loose but snug, and swung up.

Rezin walked over, caught the reins of the grulla, and stood there in the sheen of pale light, looking up at her. She nodded to him without another word, and nudged the mare. He watched her go several yards before he spoke.

"Dawn, Faith. At the Hartman place."

If she heard, she gave no sign. He watched her disappear into the late night, squatted, and rolled a cigarette, more perturbed now than ever.

The tiny glow of his quirly flashed fitfully as he smoked and thought. It was a little beacon that could be seen for a long way, providing anyone was looking at it, but the six CL riders riding over the range toward home were neither looking for a man smoking on the ground beside his horse nor even conscious that such a man might be near, as they proceeded through the darkness a quarter mile away.

It wasn't until a horseshoe *splanged* off a piece of granite that Rezin thought about anyone else but Faith Lewis. Then he arose warily, grinding out his tell-tale cigarette under a boot heel, and turned toward the sound, with one hand going to the ridgling's nose. The grulla had turned his head, pointed his ears. He couldn't see them, but the smell came downwind to him, just as the sound of steel on rock had come to his master.

Rezin mounted quickly and sat like a statue, peering into the night. Faintly, by straining, he could make out other little sounds, like rein chains and spur rowels, and the garrulous squeak of tack that hadn't been oiled.

He waited until the riders had gone by, then reined in behind them, keeping a prudent distance until he saw them go down the dark, shadowy lane of the CL and emerge into the light-washed yard, where someone brought a lantern out of the barn while they unsaddled. He counted them, and knew the entire CL crew had been abroad. It made him wonder uneasily what else was happening in the gloom of the sullen darkness.

Scowling, he reined back toward the Hartman place, but stopped at the furry edge of Razorback and dismounted. Something big was afoot, and somehow, some way, he felt like he was unknowingly the vortex of it. The dim paleness of the old log barn and house, so patiently waiting and bleached by the elements, were barely discernible ahead of him. He looked at them with a brooding attention and thought what they should look like, except for the guns of murderers. He made a hard face and thought of Burt Hunt's reticence in telling him, years before, who had signed the deed transferring the Hartman holdings to the CL. Well, that man had paid, if not in full at least with his life. Bull Antrim might have recognized the man who had killed him.

Then he wondered if Burt had been telling the truth when he steadfastly said he had no idea who the other man was—only that Antrim had winked at him tauntingly, and told him his partner wouldn't sign. He was a silent partner. That mystery had plagued Rezin for many years. He had always thought the other man must be Cliff Lewis. Now he wondered.

In some ways he wished he had caught Bull out, alone, and forced the truth out of him. But Burt had said you might kill Antrim, but you'd never get him to say anything he didn't want to say. Rezin smiled harshly. Well, Antrim hadn't been tested, so neither he nor Burt would ever know, now, about Antrim's stubbornness.

Rezin was too far away to have heard Owl Russel's stolen horse loping easily back toward Buckrum. The simple reason that he didn't hear it—when Owl tired of waiting for dawn and was half sick from the jerking nerves that were crawling under his hide—was because he was too far away from the CL headquarters when Owl rode off.

Owl was worried for the first time since he had first hired out the ivory-butted guns for gold. He had never been caught so far from safety before, never been so badly outmaneuvered, or allowed himself to become the hunted instead of the hunter. The jagged little thought he'd had earlier persisted. He was cracking. The indomitable iron shell was giving way.

He made up his mind as he rode. He'd clean out Conseil Purdy and slope. He laughed drunkenly, shrilly, into the darkness as he rode along. He let the laughter die and reached down to scratch his ribs, where they crawled with fire. *Gotta quit. Gotta rest for a while. A long, long while. Stop these things from eating into my guts.*

The black eyes were wide and peopled the night

with a small host of white faces jouncing over the range with him. Looking over at him, smiling evilly, anticipating and hopeful. He cursed them vigorously. There was that freighter who'd hired out to the Army to conceal the Fort Blevins' payroll under his load because a killer was marauding the trail. There was that dispatch carrier who he'd thought was packing money to Carson's column, and the would-be gunman from Taos.

Farther out, apart from the others, and always just a little ahead of the stud's sweaty forehead, half effaced by the tossing forelock, was Celeste Mirabeaux. He swore at the others and dared them to come closer. All of them, even the ones he barely recalled and those he'd forgotten completely. But he tried his best to ignore Celeste, and, while he did, each line of her face became clearer and clearer. He remembered that night she'd fought him. He turned away from the others, looked straight at her, and couldn't think of a thing to say that would rise over the sobs.

He gouged the big roan brutally and felt the animal race out, but the faces kept pace. He couldn't outrun them, although he tried all the way to Buckrum, and reined up only when the one or two lights shone ahead of him on the prairie. Then caution came up.

Buckrum was asleep. Even the tension and excitement and whispers that had overwhelmed the little town had been put to bed. The townsmen had retired, and the cowboys had loped back to the ranches. Owl unsaddled the spent stallion and turned him loose, abandoning him. A twinge of remorse went over him at sight of the nearly wind-broken animal.

He was careful in his approach to town. He thought of Liza, and frowned. Later, after he'd settled with Conseil Purdy.

A pleasant thought struck him as he went down the alley behind the Parker House. He'd go elsewhere and rest for a long time. He had plenty of money, and needed only one thing to make a hide-out complete. Liza. He'd take her along, too. The wonder of the idea made him flush with pleasure.

Maybe they'd go back to the Siwash teepees of the high uplands and live with the Indians. It was a good, free life. Maybe, even, he'd turn trader. He'd tried it once, and made money. Not fast enough, but still, things were different now. He didn't need money so much any more. What he needed now was a long rest.

Owl Russel was almost his old self by the time he reached the back door to the Parker House kitchen. The faces were gone, but the crawling inside his skin wasn't. He pushed inside, saw the wrinkled, bleary-eyed old swamper mopping the floor, tiptoed past him unseen, and walked across the deserted rooms. He came to the rank smell of the saloon, where only one small night lamp burned sullenly on the back bar, under the stuffed bird. It threw his shadow, tremendously large and palpitating, on the smoke-darkened ceiling overhead. He looked down, saw what he was looking for. The thin sliver of light under Purdy's office door. He went over and knuckled it gently. The tight fear in the voice that challenged him brought back a shredded piece of his old contempt.

"Who's there?"

"Open up."

A small tin can lid tacked over a smaller hole in the door slid sideways, and Purdy's bloodshot eye looked out, hesitated suspiciously, and blinked. "What you want? You get him?"

The fire was banked against Owl's soul again. He didn't answer. The doorknob turned to the lock and turned no farther. Owl's shoulder hit the panel. It groaned, and Purdy squeaked inside as he scuttled away.

Again and again, then the lock tore out of the wood and crashed inward, and Owl was looking at Purdy who was squatting in his chair by the desk, pale and shaking badly. Owl pushed the door closed, turned, regarded Purdy somberly, went over, and sat down in a chair by the big safe.

"Got whiskey?"

Purdy motioned to a table behind the chair, up against the wall and the safe. Owl turned, saw the half empty bottle, pulled it to him, uncorked it, and drank twice without lowering the bottle. He let it lie in his lap, and felt the warmth spread downward until the little crawling things were pushed down lower, to wherever they lived inside of him.

He looked at Purdy's contorted face and saw the

cocked six-gun he was holding for the first time. He laughed, drank again, and laughed again.

"You yellow buzzard." The crawlers were completely gone. He felt normal again, and relaxed. Even a little tired. "I still haven't got him. He's the first ever kept me waiting so long. I don't like it." He shifted a little in the chair. "Where's that poker-faced sheriff?"

Purdy shook his head. "Don't know. Haven't seen him since he herded the CL out of here."

Owl shrugged. "Don't matter. Don't like it, though, the way he stares all the time and says nothing."

Purdy's fear was diluted with plain logic that told him, if the gun hawk would come back to kill him, at least it wasn't going to happen for a while.

"You'll like it less if someone saw you come in here. The whole countryside's after you."

Owl drank again, slower. "I'm going to leave." He motioned with his disengaged hand toward the huge old safe. "Gimme half of what's in there."

Purdy's finger was tightening around the trigger inside the very small trigger guard. "Not on your life."

Owl looked at him with distorted vision that showed two people. One was Conseil Purdy sitting in the chair holding a gun on him. The other was a reeling squaw standing just behind the chair. He nodded thoughtfully.

"Purdy?! I like Pardeu better. Conseil Pardeu." He watched the face blanch a little across the room from him. "Conseil Pardeu, the trapper and trader. You know what that name reminds me of? Of a *hombre* who clubbed two Siwash squaws to death and stole their bundles of pelts." The handsome dark head rocked back and forth as Owl shrugged. "Don't worry. It don't make a damned bit of difference to me, only, by God, I want some more money to get away on. Now!"

The black eyes were turning vicious. Owl had another short drink. That one was from habit. Conseil Purdy was chewing low, along the right-hand side of his mouth, over toward the corner where the lips came together. It drew his face downward. Something incredulous was in his eyes. The gun sagged. He nodded dreamily. "All right. To go away on."

Owl nodded. Purdy fished out his big wallet from inside his coat, one-handed. He opened it on the desk and fished out a thick sheaf of paper money, hundreds of dollars, rolled them around, and tossed the bundle to Russel. "To go away on," he repeated.

Owl caught the money, felt it, and stuffed it into his shirt. He looked broodingly at Purdy, set the whiskey bottle down, got up, and walked out without a backward glance. The old contempt, blown to vast proportions, warmed him.

He stood in the stillness of the saloon, went over behind the bar, made a sour mash, triple size, drank it, fought back the tears, and stalked out of the place. He had completely forgotten Liza.

Just one more thing to do. He was his old self again. That called for vindication of his panic earlier, that had made him flee like a yellow cur. Kill Rezin Hartman. Hartman—that meant the old ranch again. He'd go back there.

He went out into the darkness and didn't feel the chill that had come with the pre-dawn. He'd ride a real horse, this time.

Cleat was snoring too loudly to hear the spurs come into the office. Owl wrinkled his nose at the fecal odor of the old man. He pulled down his rig and saddled up carelessly, right under the lantern, swung up, and jogged north until he was clear of town, then south-west. He thought of the green-eyed girl then, and cursed that he had forgotten Liza. Maybe, afterwards, he'd risk one more trip to Buckrum. If his mind hadn't been awry, he would have known better. He thought of the Lewis girl. She'd be closer, anyway.

Faith waited in the living room for Cliff to enter. She heard his spurs on the verandah, stiffened, and saw him come through the screen door.

He stopped just inside, regarded her owlishly, dumped his hat on the table, and sat down. She didn't move. He ran a tired hand through his mop of hair and flagged her toward a chair.

"Sit down, honey. I've got a story to tell you." She hesitated. He wrinkled his forehead irritably. "Sit down!" She sat.

Cliff rolled a cigarette, trying to bring the whole thing into better focus before he spoke. He lit it, inhaled, and leaned back. His back had been bothering him a little lately.

"I got to go back a ways. This'll be something you probably won't understand. The Brazitos hasn't always been orderly like it is now. The first few years we were here . . . your mother and me . . . things were pretty wild. There was broncho Injuns coming through every now and then, and passels of raiding Mexicans, and all sorts of renegades. Rustlers and the like."

He was looking at her, but past her, too. "Them days, Faith, 'twasn't anything to see six, eight two-gun men in Buckrum. Things were pretty wild. We kept to ourselves and worked . . . your mother and me . . . then she got the fever and passed on." He paused for a second there, then continued. "If you're wondering why I'm telling you this, it's because I want you to understand how different things was in those days, honey. So's you'll understand what I did later, and why."

Faith leaned back slowly and watched her father. He wasn't looking at her at all, then. His gaze was fastened on a mothy old golden grizzly skin that had hung on the south wall of the parlor for as long as she could remember.

"Well . . . after your mother passed away, I still kept on. Don't ask me why. I'll be darned if I know. Maybe because I figured you'd want this someday. Maybe because it was habit by then to work all the time. Anyway, she and me started it together, so I kept on."

He brought his glance down off the wall and looked straight at Faith. "Don't make no difference now, anyway, does it?"

Faith didn't answer. She was picturing him thirty years before. Big, brawny, shrewd, and brave as a lion. Respected even in the lawlessness of the early days, and left alone. He ran the same hand through his hair again.

"All right. That'll put us about fifteen years back by now. There was some other settlers in the country then, too. Not many, but a few. They all were starting cow outfits. A lot of them got cleaned out or shot down, or just give up and went back where they came from. It was a hard country then, honey. You'll never know. Maybe you'll never understand, either." He shrugged. "That's what I'm trying to tell you . . . to say . . . that Buckrum them days had no law. Only gun law. We had a constable once, but he got hung later for stealing horses. Anyway, there were these other settlers, too. I'm the only one left, now, of the original folks who settled here. Just about.

"There was a big, bearded *hombre* and his wife . . . real pretty she was, too, with bronze-gold sort of hair. They took up land west of us. We used to visit back and forth a little, and he helped me build the barn and this very house. He had a gift with his hands. Never seen another man like him."

Faith interrupted. "Was his name . . . Hartman?"

"Yes."

Cliff acted like the name wasn't pleasant to him.

"Yes, his name was Birch Hartman. Her name was Tamsen." He let his eyes run to a darkened corner of the old room, where a weathered string instrument of ancient design leaned against the wall.

"See that dulcimer there? That one that Maria used to give you the dickens for playing with? Well, later, I brought it over here, from the old house. Couldn't none of the CL play it, but Tamsen Hartman played it for Birch and me many's the night. Sometimes I can hear it now."

"Was she pretty, Dad? I mean, did she have nice manners and . . . and . . . ?"

"Prettiest lady I ever seen, outside of your mother." Cliff wanted to get off the subject of the murdered woman, but still it brought back so many things he cherished inside, and in going forward would resurrect other things, too, that were nostalgically pleasant, that it was a sort of sweet pain to him. He sighed and stretched out his legs, crossing one spurred boot over the other. The night was still as a tomb.

"I hadn't seen Birch or his wife for several months. Things were like that. I was running a cow ranch, and busy from dawn until dark. Anyway, we didn't go calling them days, like folks do nowadays."

He paused, took it up again with an effort, and went on.

"One morning about sunup, I heard someone drive a rig into the yard, and went out. There was a man coming across the yard toward me, so I waited. The other one . . . the man still in the buggy . . . never got down, and to this day I don't know who he was. Anyway, this here *hombre* comes up and nods. He says . . . 'Mister Lewis, I got a piece of land for sale that adjoins you to the west. Would you be interested in buying it?' Faith, that's the only way to get a big cow outfit. Buy your land. Don't let these smart alecks tell you otherwise. I've seen lots of them come and go in the Brazitos because they wouldn't buy what they got to use free. It was a mistake. Both your mother and I knew it.

"This here's good land. Someday someone'll buy every open section. That's why I'm still here after the others're gone. And it's also why I've got the biggest and best ranch in the territory."

His eyes were glinting with conviction. She understood what had been behind his driving urge all these years, and admired it.

"Well, sir, I asked this man his name. He said Bull Antrim. Then I asked him what land he owned, since I'd never heard of him before. He told me it was the Hartman place. I thought he was crazy, or drunk. Birch and me saw eye to eye on getting good land and holding it. Now, here was a stranger offering to sell me Hartman's ranch. I told him he must be mistaken, and he ups and gives me a recorded deed to the place to look at."

Cliff's eyes were watching Faith closely. "I told him I'd think it over and meet him in town later on. At first, I figured Birch'd just got tired of bucking the land and give up like the others. Then I wondered.

Anyway . . . I rode into Buckrum and met Antrim at the abstract office and heard the news. Birch and Tamsen'd been killed by Injuns. I was dumbfounded. Seemed like it had happened a few weeks before. I didn't hardly ever go to town and hadn't visited them for several months. I had a few drinks, and thought it over. At that time I figured this here Antrim was some sort of relative come to settle their affairs. I bought the place, and sat right in Burt Hunt's office . . . he was Tamsen's brother . . . while that yellow-bellied buzzard recorded my new deed and give me the papers.

"Never could stand the sight of Burt after that. His own sister, and he had to know something was wrong when this Antrim had the deed, but he never said a word. Just made out the papers and give me title to the Hartman place." Cliff was frowning fiercely as he relived those moments. "Like I said, I didn't hang out in town much, and first I didn't hear the talk. Folks'd left off saying the Injuns had killed the Hartmans and were saying Cliff Lewis'd done it so's he'd get their land. They said the proof was that I'd bought the place. Well, now, honey, I never killed a man that didn't need killing, and, by God, I've never drawn a gun on a woman in my life. No matter what she done. And . . . when I was young, there was some that did me no favors. Now, Faith, like I told you, them days it was a wild country. At first I was mad as hell that folks'd say I killed the Hartmans. Then I noticed that whenever my land touched someone else's, they get uneasy and, sooner or later, ask me if I'd like to buy them out. I looked at it like this. I had the name, although I swear to you I had nothing to do with those killings, but why . . . if I was branded a murderer, and folks was leery of me . . . why, then, shouldn't I profit from it?"

He saw the cloudy look on her face. "That's the hardest part, Faith. Y'see, you can't understand a thing like that. Times have changed."

He took a long, last draw on his cigarette, and tossed it into the black fireplace hole. "So I bought the others out as they come to me, and that's how the CL came to be what it is today."

Cliff stopped talking, cleared his throat, spat into the fireplace, and leaned back in the chair again.

"I often wondered who this Antrim was. He came to me for a job about twelve years ago. He'd settled in Buckrum. Well, I hired the man, and finally he got to be foreman as others rode on. Oh, Bull wasn't the best stockman, but the rustling stopped and folks stepped light around the CL after he come to work for me."

Faith shook her head. "Where did Bull get the deed?"

Cliff paused again. "That's something else I don't like talking about. It makes me out in a sort of poor light. Faith, I give you my word, I never asked him. Personal questions, them days, honey, was something you just didn't ask a man." Cliff switched the upper foot under the lower one. It was going to sleep. "I always figured someday I'd ask him about that deed." He shrugged. "Close to fifteen years I knew Bull pretty well, and never did I get so's I figured I knew him well enough to ask. Oh, I reckoned to ask him, sometime, if I ever got a good chance. I figured he could tell me more about the passing of the Hartmans than anyone else. That is, if he knew anything at all. But I just never got the chance."

"But Dad, why didn't you ask Burt Hunt? Surely he . . . ?"

Cliff snorted in great disgust. "That chicken-livered old . . . old whelp! He's a coward from the word go." He looked at her speculatively, seemed to be considering something, then spoke. "I'll tell you something about Burt. There used to be a feller run a saloon here in Buckrum. He's that tramp that's Ed Smith's hostler at the livery barn now. *Hombre* by the name of Cleat Stuart. Him and Burt were soldiers together in the Rebel Army. He told me that Burt got a yellow discharge. That means he was a coward." Cliff blinked in scorn. "Bad enough, he was a Rebel, but a yellow discharge. Nothing worse, to my notions." He jerked his head irritably. "Burt'd do anything to avoid trouble. Even cover up his own sister's murder, mind you."

Faith sighed. She was almost overcome with fatigue and sadness. The sky was beginning to lighten along the flat planes of the horizon, like the earth was square, and a blue fire was burning just below its farthest rim. She looked out the window just as a rooster crowed out in back of the house somewhere.

"Then, really, the Hartman's place belonged to their little boy."

196

Cliff nodded slowly. "I reckon."

She looked back at him. "You *reckon?* You know darned well it does. He was their heir, wasn't he?"

Cliff squirmed. "Well, I didn't know what happened to the kid. They had a Injun orphan they'd picked up somewhere, too. All I knew was that he disappeared right after the killings."

"You didn't ask?"

Cliff looked strained. "Listen, Faith. I had other things to worry about than stray kids. Like I said before, them days. . . ."

"Were different," she finished softly. "I guess they were. Nothing seemed to matter much, then, except coming out on top. Did it?"

"No. That and keeping your hair on top of your head, and keeping some marauding buzzards from rustling you broke, and holding what you'd got so's, someday, you'd have your own empire. That's about all, and it wasn't no cinch. You ask any of the old-timers . . . the ones that's still here, anyway."

"Oh, Dad, in a way I'm awfully relieved. In another way, it makes me feel sad." She let her eyes wander over the staid solidness of the big room, with its droopy, old, Indian trophies—and the lonely dulcimer in the corner—gathering decades of forgotten dust.

Cliff nodded. He understood better than she would ever have believed. No man's so hard that the years don't teach him mellowness from the lessons of his memories. "Yes, honey, I know." He sat for a long time in silence, then framed the only question that still remained unanswered. "Do you understand, Faith, what I've done, and why I did it?"

"Yes, I suppose so, Dad. It's like you say. Things were so awfully different then." She thought of the way Rezin had held her when she'd had hysterics. "But what about Rezin?"

"Rezin?" He pulled his thoughts back with a visible effort. "Oh, Hartman." He blinked suddenly. "Rezin? Faith, do you know him?"

She nodded gently. "Yes, Dad."

"Oh!" He looked at her and drummed on the leather arm of his chair. Here was something else coming at him. He felt like he'd like nothing better, right then, than just to saddle up a horse and ride away. Turn his back on the whole bitter monument of his past—and the sorry present, too. Things were happening too fast. Too suddenly and harshly. Maybe she didn't see what was ahead, but he did.

"I don't know. I'll find him, I reckon. If Dex doesn't get him first, and try to explain it all to him." He shoved himself upright, suddenly, out of the chair. "I'll give him back the Hartman place. I reckon that ought to square things." He frowned. "When he killed Bull . . . I wonder . . . did he know something? Or did he do it just because Bull had sort of robbed him of his birthright?" He was watching Faith closely. If she knew Hartman, maybe he'd talked to her. She shrugged and met the glance. He knew she didn't have the answer, even before she spoke.

"I don't know, Dad. But he's . . . well . . . he doesn't

impress me as the type who'd kill a man just on suspicion."

Cliff wanted to deride that with his impatient snort. He'd lived a lot longer, and knew a lot better. He didn't make a sound, though, just rose to his feet. Faith got up and went over to him. She tiptoed as far as she could, reached and kissed him on one leathery cheek, where the beard stubble was beginning to show, stiff and white.

"I'm awfully sorry, Dad. Awfully."

Cliff patted her. "Go to bed, honey. It's almost dawn. Will be in another hour or so. Get some sleep. We'll hunt up your Hartman boy t'morrow."

He patted her again, ruffled the hair clumsily, like he did ten years before when she was trying to look very feminine, and remembered how her green eyes would snap at him in anger.

"G'night, Faith."

" 'Night, Dad."

Chapter Six
DAWN AT HARTMAN'S

Sheriff Dexter Williams scratched his head and smiled dolefully. "Well, I reckon Con'll make all profit off that room of mine tonight."

Berl nodded as they went over the still land. "Me, too. I'd like to stop off right here and sleep for a year."

Dexter nodded sympathetically, but his next words

showed that he wasn't thinking about rest. "What's Faith got to do with this mess, anyway? Why'd she and Cliff have a fight?"

"That's easy," Berl said. "He was sore because she warned off Hartman. I reckon the girl's got a lot of the old man in her, too. She blew up and left home."

Dexter rode slowly, wrapped in silence, and turned it over carefully before he agreed. "You're right. Sure as God made green apples. Should've seen it myself. Getting logy, I reckon."

Berl reined up. "Let's have your tobacco sack. Never could stand chewing before dawn."

Dexter reined up, handed his sack and papers over, watched Berl make a quirly, then rolled one himself. They were both sucking smoke into their lungs, with Berl making a face, when a noise came out of the night to them. Dexter cupped his cigarette and listened.

"Rider behind us somewhere."

"Yeah. But which way is he going?"

Dexter was silent for a long moment, then he frowned. "Coming this way, Berl."

The deputy shook his head exasperatedly. "What's the matter with folks, anyway? They forgot what beds are for?"

"Don't make a bobble. He's going to pass us to the north."

Berl strained his weary eyes, squinted hard, and touched the sheriff's sleeve lightly after the stranger had gone by. "I'll be darned, Dex. You see him?"

"Yeah. I saw him, but not well enough to know who it was. Did you?"

"Yeah."

"Who?"

"I may be loco, but I'll swear it was Con Purdy packing a carbine in his lap."

Dexter looked amazed. "You *must* be loco. I've known Con a long time, and I've never seen him ride a horse."

Berl nodded his head doggedly. "Well . . . I'll still say it was Con." He shook his reins. "Let's catch up and make sure."

Dexter shook his head. "No. Let him go. I got a feeling. Just let him go, Berl."

"Why? He's got a rifle."

"That's just it. We know he and that 'breed are tied in some way. Con packing a rifle and riding the night might mean they're going to meet. We'll just follow him and nab our 'breed gunman, see?"

Berl smiled and smoked as they rode forward again. "You're pretty smart at that, Dex. Considering your age and all."

Dexter's tart and pointed answer brought a gleeful chuckle from the deputy. They rode on, barely keeping the wraith-like specter ahead of them in sight.

Purdy was riding like a man immersed in his own frantic thoughts, which he was. There was a light pinkish cast to the saliva that moistened his mouth, where he'd finally bitten into the quick and made his cheek lining bleed. A jungle of disjointed thoughts ached behind his forehead, the least of which was the frightened, startled look on Cleat's puffy face when Purdy had saddled up, dragged the rifle up into the saddle with him, and ridden out of Buckrum.

The other thoughts were dredged up out of a long string of yesterdays. Some of them were very dim and muddy, with indistinct features that blurred constantly. He recognized each one, though, and they all added up to a very necessary killing. Rezin Hartman's killing. The years had robbed him of the heart for the chore, but not the determination. He jogged along through the night, knowing inwardly that Owl Russel's defeat and rout hadn't been altogether the gunman's fault alone. There was something else—medicine, the Siwash would call it—aiding this son of murdered parents.

Purdy's eyes glistened in the darkness. Well, he had strong medicine, too. One or the other would prove the stronger. He was prepared both ways. The rifle in his lap one way, the pepperbox .41 caliber in his coat pocket the other way. Purdy had no idea where he'd find his victim. Something had told him to ride to the abandoned old Hartman ranch, and he fell in with it.

Like Owl—but without knowing it—he had reasoned that Hartman, if still in the country, would be drawn toward the home he was born in, where the spirits of his people still were. Purdy had a lot in common with Owl Russel—and he didn't know that, either. Owl did, though.

"Which way's he going?"

"Looks to me like the CL, Berl."

"Maybe him and old Cliff are in cahoots, some way."

Dexter snorted. "I just can't see that. They got about as much in common as . . . as . . . you and that 'breed two-gun man."

"Where'd you suppose that crazy buzzard went?"

"I'll bet he's either a long way off or darned close. One or the other."

Berl spat and looked over at Dexter's silhouette a few feet away. "Well . . . ain't that bright? He's either underfoot or not underfoot." The sarcasm was almost tangible.

Dexter shook his head. "I mean, he's either scairt plumb out of the Brazitos, or he's holed up somewhere waiting to get in his licks. Hell . . . for all we know, he may be stalking the CL, waiting for a chance to get at Faith again."

"No," Berl said emphatically. "He's not that stupid. He'd never live to ride away, come daylight. Old Cliff'd see him ten miles away over the CL range. No cover that far for a rider." He shook his head. "I think he's left the country by now. I would've, if the CL was hot after me like they are for him."

"I reckon. But I got a feeling . . . just a feeling, that's all."

Berl spat again. The inside of his mouth was sour

and tasted coated. "Well, in a way, I hope you're right. I'd like to get a shot at him myself. Just one shot."

"Hey," Dexter said, impressed. "It's darned near dawn. Look off over there."

Berl didn't look. "I know it. I can feel the chill in the air, not to mention my whiskers and the taste in my mouth. You still see Con?"

"No. Don't see him, but I know he's up ahead by the sounds."

"Which way's he going? Still toward the CL?"

"No, toward the old Hartman place."

"The devil! That darned ruin's had more company in the last two days than it's had in years."

"Yeah," the sheriff agreed. "Well . . . maybe we can get some idea about what happened to the Hartmans, too. I got a feeling this Rezin *hombre* has stirred up a hornet's nest, and we'll learn something from it."

"If we don't get stung, too," Berl said dryly.

"Con's sure riding slow. If I was going somewhere with a rifle on my saddle, I'd want to get it over with, or get the devil away from it."

Berl spat again, made a grimace, and didn't speak. His teeth felt like they'd sprouted fur.

As they swung past the dim trail to the CL and headed southwest, the sheriff thought of Faith Lewis. He couldn't figure her part in the trouble. She was so pretty and naïve-appearing. He looked in the direction of the CL buildings, couldn't see anything, and pictured Faith in his mind. He sighed a little. Were he a younger man, he'd have thought about her seriously.

• • •

The girl sat for a full hour, and longer, in her leather chair, until she was sure Cliff would be sleeping. Then she got up and tiptoed out of the house, went down to the barn, and saddled her chestnut mare.

The trail around Razorback was eerie in the gloom. She rode it slowly, toward the old Hartman place. Dawn wasn't far off. She could smell it, cool and sharp, in the air. Some aroused birds chirped drowsily, irritably, in the edge of some brush as she rode by.

In spite of the dreariness that oppressed her body, her spirit was lifted—poignantly, perhaps—but still lifted. Her father hadn't been in on the murders at all. It bothered her that she'd thought he had. But, knowing Cliff Lewis, it was hard to decide just where he would draw the line, because he was as hard as granite and difficult to understand.

It was a small consolation to Faith, too, that she had thought her father capable of murdering another man and his wife, until she remembered that it wasn't so much that she'd thought he had as it was the wonder if he had. She sighed and pushed the guilt sense and the fatigue away, and thought of Rezin.

That first kiss could have been prompted by anything. Hate even. It had shaken her often when she had thought of it, but not nearly as badly as this other one, last night—or this morning, whichever it was. That one had had substance and understanding behind it, even if his hate trail was admittedly stronger. She let her mind wander on about him. The bronze-gold hair. The clear blue eyes that had such startlingly whites. The lean, sinewy arms and shoulders under that dirty shirt. His laugh was good to remember, too. The way it started in a slow smile, then a chuckle, then the laughter itself. It made her smile a little. Such an odd way to laugh. Like it was begrudging and built around some humorous momentum that gathered way slowly. Which was exactly the way it was, with Rezin. Faith had unconsciously learned to know him better than she thought—or realized.

She came around the edge of Razorback and swung down the cattle trail, letting her mare pick the way. The animal knew where she was going, and did the job well. The ghostly outline of the buildings loomed up in the near distance before Faith sighed, forced herself erect, and ran thoughtful fingers through her hair and forced the long strands under the little ribbon, pulled it tighter, and re-settled her hat. Slouching forward again in the saddle, she rode up to, and through, the gate hole. She reined in then, wondering what to do next.

She didn't have long to wonder. Rezin came out of the shadows from the box spring without speaking. He walked up close to her, put a hand on her leg, and held out the other hand.

She leaned forward, grasped the hand, and swung down. He reached over and loosened her saddle cinch, looped the reins, and turned back where Faith was walking over toward the broken door stoop. He followed her and sat down beside her, running a self-conscious hand over the bristle on his face.

"Well?"

"Well, I know enough to tell you my dad didn't have any part of the actual killings."

"No?" Rezin was inwardly glad and relieved—if it was true.

"No." She didn't look at him as she talked. She went back to her first accusation of her father. The way she had left the CL, and why. She even told him about Owl Russel's part in her leaving home. Then, gradually, she worked back to what her father had told her. It sounded vindicating in her own ears as she told it.

Rezin listened with his head back, eyes looking off toward the weak light that was getting stronger in a blue-gray way. Then she finished speaking and looked over at his profile.

"Well?" she said.

"All right, Faith. I didn't think you'd do it, though."

"What? Find out from Dad what happened?"

"Yes." He turned and looked down at her, saw the way her youth was sagging, slack-muscled from exhaustion, and knew how she'd look at forty. It still looked very good to him. He sighed.

"Honey, that only proved one thing. That Cliff Lewis didn't kill them. Then who did?"

"I don't know. Couldn't your Uncle Burt say? Doesn't he have any ideas?"

Rezin shook his head. "No, I'm sure he doesn't. No matter what Burt is . . . and I have my own ideas on the subject . . . he's always been very good to me. Had me boarded out and sent to school, and all that." He shrugged. "Maybe that's his way of paying back his conscience for not going after his sister's killers. I don't know. Anyway . . . whatever he is, he's not a liar. He told me he had no idea who the other one was, and I believe him. He didn't know. Your pa doesn't know. So that leaves me just about where I was. All I do know is that Cliff Lewis wasn't one of them."

Faith leaned back against the old log wall with a solemn look. "Rezin . . . if Dad gave you back the Hartman place and let you set it up, even helped you, wouldn't that make a difference?"

He looked at her in silence.

She returned the glance soberly, and spoke again without even trying to fathom the strange look on his face. "I mean, he'd give you interest for the years in cattle. I know he would. You could fix the house up again. It's really not in bad shape." She remembered what her father had said about Birch Hartman's having great skill with his hands, and knew, all of a sudden, why the Hartman place still stood, true and sound as when it had been built, when so many of the other old ranch buildings had crumbled and fallen. "Oh, there'd always be the sorrow, Rezin. I understand that. But wouldn't it be better if you got the ranch back and re-stocked with cattle . . . and all?" She watched his eyes for a change, saw none, and gave it up after a parting volley. "You've gotten the most important one. Bull Antrim paid you. It'll be hard . . .

maybe impossible ever to find the other one." She pushed off the wall and leaned forward, pulling her knees up and clasping them with her arms, looking at him. "If you go on this way, Rezin, you might kill the wrong man. You almost did, anyway, y'know. You even had me half believing Dad was a murderer. Please, Rezin. You've done enough, and . . . and besides. . . ."

"Yes?"

"Nothing. Only remember, the next man may be a better shot than Bull was."

"Honey, it's fixing to break day. You'd better get back before your pa wakes up and misses you."

"Well, will you do that? Will you forget it now, and let Dad . . . ?"

"I'm sorry, Faith." He added nothing to it. She understood, got up slowly, and walked over by her mare, tightened the cinch with blurred vision, turned the mare a little, and swung up. He had come up beside her, stood at the mare's shoulder, and looked up at her. She leaned down sideways.

"Rezin . . . I'll come back tonight . . . if you want me to."

"Honey, if I just knew who the other one was, believe me, I'd settle it fast. Then . . . well, then things'd be different."

"What do you mean . . . different?"

"I mean about fixing up the old Hartman place and taking cattle from your pa for the interest, and . . . and . . . well, other things."

"Then you won't leave your private hate trail until you know who the other murderer was?"

"No, Faith, I can't. Brazitos law's not interested. Never was. That leaves it up to me. You'd do the same thing, honey. Anyone would. If the law doesn't hunt down murderers, then it's up to others to do it. You can see that, can't you?"

She didn't answer. Impulsively her hand went down and flicked his hat off. It fell back into the trampled grass. Her fingers went through the thick bronze-gold hair. She knew the violent smoldering inside of her was her destiny. She knew it as instinctively as a female mountain lion, or a female wolf. It was the source and purpose of her existence.

They were too absorbed in themselves to feel the strangeness in the air, or notice how the chestnut mare's ears were pointing forward and her eyes were watching a stalwart shadow at the far end of the house, over by the box spring, the dark, handsome shadow that had come out of the old barn when he had first heard her ride up.

Owl was surprised to see her again. He was more surprised to see Rezin Hartman. Then he had listened to the last half of their conversation, and the whole sordid thing became clear to him. Not that he cared. He didn't. It was just the oddity of all this intrigue that had aroused his curiosity.

They weren't aware of anyone else in the whole world, until that third voice invaded their obliviousness.

"Is a thousand dollars, gold, too much, *hombre?*"

Rezin turned and sucked in his breath. He recognized the dark silhouette in the darkness.

"I'll sell you that information, gunman, if you want it. Thousand gold."

Faith was thunderstruck to see her late escort standing there, arms hanging at akimbo, legs spread, the brilliant black eyes on Rezin, opaque and glittering.

"What do you know?"

Owl's eyes didn't flicker. This amused him a little. Besides, it would soon be light, too light to get clear of the damned Brazitos. So he'd have to hide for the rest of the day and ride later. In the meantime, he'd make this Rezin Hartman *hombre* sweat blood. He liked the thought of Hartman's being told who the other murderer of his folks was, because he'd take the knowledge to hell with him. He'd know it too late to do anything about it. That was the best part of it. He'd killed before, trying to find out who the killers were. Now Owl Russel would tell him, watch the bitterness eat into him like corrosive acid, then kill him. That would pay him off for the beating, for the trouble and risk in hunting him down.

"You killed a *hombre* named Antrim. He had a hand in the killing of your folks. There was another one in it, too. I know who he was. I know a lot of things about this killing. Just tell me one thing, and I'll have it all. Did this Hartman *hombre* have a Injun kid around the place, working for him? A Digger?"

Rezin started. He had forgotten until just then that his father had had an Indian boy who did the chores. He dimly recalled the way the Indian and he had played together when they were small.

He nodded. "By God, yes!"

Owl Russel's head inclined slightly. "That's it, then."

"What?"

"I killed the Digger the same day you killed Antrim. The Digger was forgot when Antrim come up dead."

"Why'd you kill him?"

"For money. What else?"

Rezin was staring at Owl. His head almost ached from trying to catch the elusive little something that was all he needed. He could sense it without being able to grasp it.

"That was the Indian kid who worked for my pa?"

"Yeah."

"This other thing. Who was the other man?"

Owl's eyes were wide in his immobile face. "I'll tell you, cowboy. It won't even cost you the thousand dollars. I'll tell you because you're going to hell knowing who he was and not being able to do something about it." He canted his head a little. "Send her away. Just you and I are going to know this, so send her away."

Rezin spoke over his shoulder to Faith. "Ride off, honey. It'll be better that way. Just ride over the range a ways. Safer, too."

"No, I won't. Rezin, please!" She looked over at Owl. "Don't . . . there's been too much killing already.

Please . . . the noise'll bring the CL. Besides, you can't get away. It's breaking daylight. You'll never get away if you kill him!"

Owl's eyes never left Rezin's face. "Go on. I'll tend to you later. You and me are going to talk about you leaving the hotel."

"Shut your mouth!"

Owl did, but because of the fierceness in Rezin's voice, not because of the command. He studied the man standing beside the chestnut mare intently. It was time now. The sun was just showing, an inverted, brassy piece of molten metal, over the edge of the horizon.

"All right cowboy. The other one was Con Purdy. Only that's not his name. Don't make no difference. You know him as Con Purdy. He hired me to kill the Digger, and he also hired me to kill you. I got real money for you. It's in my pocket now. I'd've killed you, anyway. I owe you that. Con Purdy, he was the other one with the *hombre* named Antrim. Satisfied? You know now."

Faith could sense the breaking over of the killer's intentions from one thing to another. He was through with one phase and ready to embark on the final one. She was desperate and acted on the spur of the moment.

The chestnut mare lunged with a great *whoosh* of startled breath. The spurs went deep. Someone roared a curse and a gun exploded. Then another one. She felt the mare stiffen wildly in mid-stride, then go forward on buckling legs. Two more thunderous crashes roared. Then a crazy patchwork of explosions. She lay flat where she had fallen, looking sideways at the dead mare, petrified with fear. Someone was running. A man knelt beside her, rolled her over roughly, and looked down, as white as a sheet. It was Rezin.

"Honey!" It was a whisper, hoarse and shaky. "Are you hit, Faith?" She couldn't speak, so she shook her head. Relief spread over his face. The color came back, and with it anger. "That was a fool thing to do." He bent quickly then, and planted a kiss with shockingly cold lips, then lunged to his feet, and raced around the corner of the building, where he'd left the grulla ridgling.

Owl Russel was scared. He pulled up the cinch on the big black and bridled him with shaking hands, lunged into the saddle, and roared out of the old barn, sending a blind shot down toward the house. Just before the barn separated him from the house, he caught a flashing glimpse of Rezin, throwing his saddle on the grulla. It made him thrill to the certainty of escape. Even neck and neck, he doubted if the grulla could catch his black. He still leaned forward a little, but the fear subsided a lot.

The sun was making a pink glow over the land. Owl was running for his life. He swore. Four shots, and the victim had lived to fire back at him. That had never happened before. There was sweat on his upper lip and along the ribs under his shirt. He swung around a little, although he thought any pursuit would be useless. There was none. He twisted farther around and saw something else that chilled him. Far away, clearing the lower end of Razorback in a dead run, were five or six riders. It was hard to tell because they were bunched and coming down the land like race horses, riders low and straining.

He caught the glitter of sunlight on the rifle barrels with a premonition of disaster that he couldn't shake off. Then he saw Rezin Hartman coming. He watched the grulla race over the land with mild surprise at the swirl of speed. But still he had nothing to fear. The pursuit was too far off to be dangerous, but the premonition of disaster still persisted in his chest, and finally rose into his throat.

Faith was standing by her dead horse, transfixed as she watched the CL flash by. Her father waved a gloved hand grimly, then they were gone. She swung around, saw that Rezin's horse was badly handicapped in the grim race by Owl Russel's great start and unbelievably fast black horse. She hoped Rezin wouldn't get close enough to shoot, then the fanning out CL riders obscured her vision. Little dust devils jerked to life and flung themselves upward in the air, to hang suspended for a breathless moment before they drifted back over the churned-up range.

Purdy sat perfectly still, watching the mighty black horse racing along toward him at an angle. He watched and unconsciously bit the inside of his mouth. The great disc on the far horizon was in his face, making him squint. Slowly, stiffly, he swung down, walked around in front of his horse, knelt, and levered the carbine. He watched the black horse coming up. Saw the rider twisting, looking back at the wild pursuit, then he raised his gun, poised it, lowered it again, watched the black horse for a second longer, knew he was well within range, shouldered the gun, hovered over it, and squeezed the trigger.

The blast of rifle fire rolled over and over the land, chasing itself down to the last echo. The black horse was thrown off lead by the rider's lurch. Purdy levered again, watching.

Owl felt the breathtaking shock after he heard the report. It was like a huge fist had struck him in the side. It forced his lungs to belch out their burden of air in a mighty eruption that whistled past his lips. Wild-eyed, he swung around, saw the man kneeling with the rifle, squinted, and tried to clear his vision. He looked again as he saw the rifle going up, then a blinding, awful pain shot through him. He reeled, fought to reach the saddle horn, missed it, went still lower, tried for a handful of whipping black mane, missed that, grabbed again, desperately, and felt himself falling.

Rezin had seen Purdy dismount just as he saw two other riders, not too far behind the rifleman, come racing over the land in a burst of sudden speed. He recognized the lean one as Dexter Williams and guessed the second man, shorter, a little behind, to be

Berl Clausen. He narrowed his eyes in wonder at the man who had shot Owl Russel out of the saddle. He was squatting there, the carbine hanging listlessly in his hands. It looked like Con Purdy.

Rezin saw Purdy look over at him even as he heard the pounding thunder of riders behind him. He shot a startled glance over his shoulder, saw Cliff Lewis and the CL within rifle shot, and swerved so as to get away from their charge. He didn't know what they were up to, but he didn't want them directly behind him, either. When he swerved, the carbine spat again, and the lethal whisper of a bullet went past him. Shocked, he jerked forward again, saw the kneeling man tracking him with the carbine, then the riders behind—Dexter and Berl—were flashing pistols that shot fire before the sound of the dull roars drifted down to him.

Frantic now, Rezin reined away. The morning was torn and ripped by gunfire as the CL roared past, firing wildly at the kneeling man. Rezin was horrified. The man was being hit from front and rear. Someone screamed out a string of curses. Berl and Dexter reined wildly away as CL slugs spattered the air around them. Purdy slumped forward. Rezin slowed the grulla to a long lope as he approached Owl Russel. One gun was lying where it had fallen from impact, fifteen feet from its owner. The other gun, miraculously, was still in the holster.

Rezin bent over the dying man and knelt down. One glance was enough. Rezin looked away quickly, marveling that the brilliant black eyes still held a semblance of clearness at all.

Owl read it in Rezin's face and in his squatting position, hands a long way from his guns. He blinked at the man he had wanted to kill. "Who . . . who shot me? The sheriff?"

Rezin shook his head. He had no reason to pity this man. But he did. "No, Con Purdy."

"Pardeu?" It came out with surprise and shock. "You sure?"

Rezin nodded.

Owl blinked again. "I'll be god damned!" He made a ghastly little grin. "That's . . . that's fine. That buzzard!" There was plain shock in Rezin's face. Owl saw it. "His name wasn't Purdy. It was Pardeu. Conseil Pardeu." Owl seemed to be looking inward. At least his eyes were losing their focus. "You got any colts?"

Rezin didn't know what to say. He thought Owl meant Colt guns. He was starting to nod when the man's eyes flickered, closed, and opened again as the sound of men dismounting amid the small music of their spurs came distantly to him. Rezin didn't look around. He heard Heber Kimball address Cliff Lewis in a low tone. It was the CL.

The dying man spoke again, weakly, with the salty taste of his own blood in his mouth. "Name a colt after me. Call him Owl, will you?"

Rezin nodded, saw the closed eyes, and spoke softly. "Yeah, I will."

"Listen, I got some money on me. Give it to Liza.

All of it . . . and my guns. They're good ones. Will you?"

"Sure."

Owl Russel died then, after one writhing contortion that jerked him half erect. Rezin got slowly to his feet and looked at the sober faces around him. The sheriff was just swinging down beside his deputy. They were both white-faced. He pushed past the cowboys, walked over to the grulla, swung up amid the wondering stares, and reined around, heading back toward the Hartman place. He was wearing a sick look on his face. The CL watched him go.

Dexter's mouth was a bloodless line. He ignored the dead gunman and walked up to Cliff Lewis. His eyes were glassy with fury. "You god-damned old buzzard! I ought to knock you on your. . . ."

"Hold on, Dexter!" Heber Kimball stepped in front of the angry sheriff. "What's wrong with you?"

"Listen, Heber, you crazy buzzards were shooting straight at Berl and me. Now, by God, I've had enough of the CL and its high-handedness, d'you understand? I've put up with all I'm going to stomach." He swung back to Cliff, who was stunned and wide-eyed. "I'm going to post a notice, Cliff, as soon as I get back to Buckrum. The first CL rider that shows up in town wearing a gun . . . *any* gun . . . gets thirty days in the lock-up." He let his wrath die, but the anger still showed, just below the surface. "I'm not kidding. This kind of thing's had the Brazitos scared stiff of the CL ever since I can remember. Well . . . no more. You boys remember that. All of you." He felt a little embarrassed, then, and turned to where Berl was staring dumbfounded at the wads of money he found in every pocket of the gunman.

Cliff Lewis nodded bleakly at the money in Berl's hands. "We were here when he told Hartman to give that, and his guns, to that woman who sings for . . . sang for . . . Con Purdy."

Heber Kimball walked over to Owl's black horse, stroked its sweat-streaked nose, and patted its neck. He smiled to himself, reached into a pocket, and pulled out a shabby old purse, fished out a hundred dollars, and handed it to Berl. "And this, too, Berl. That's for his horse." He jutted his chin toward the corpse. "What'll we do with him?"

Dexter shrugged. "You fellers just leave him here. The sun ain't up enough so's it's not going to bother him for an hour or two. I'll send Ed Smith's hearse out for him. At territory expense, too," he added sourly.

Cliff swallowed and turned to Dexter. "I'm sorry, Dex. I should've thought before the boys opened up."

Dexter looked his amazement. He'd known this granite-hard old man all his life. It embarrassed him to see him humbled. He cleared his throat. "Forget it, Cliff. I . . . uh . . . I only meant part of it, anyway."

Berl frowned. "Which part, Dex?"

"About them damned guns."

Cliff nodded and turned to his horse. "Let's go back to the Hartman place. Faith's over there with a dead horse."

"Yeah," Dexter said under his breath, squinting across the land as he swung up. "And that ain't all she's with, either."

Rezin watched them come, and pushed Faith away a little, flustered. She looked up at him in bewilderment.

"One minute you're telling me all sorts of things, and the next you're pushing me away."

"Yeah, I know, but they're coming over here. All of them."

She grinned through the dirt smudges on her face. "Let them come. I'm not doing anything I'm ashamed of, are you?"

"Well . . . no, not ashamed, exactly. But . . . well . . . I don't care for an audience."

"Oh, pooh!" She reached out, yanked him down by the collar and planted a kiss squarely on his mouth. He jerked back hastily and saw the grizzled old man in the lead of the astonished riders sit bolt upright in his saddle. He was sweating furiously inside his shirt and looked down at Faith reprovingly. His voice was low, but not so low Dexter Williams didn't hear it as he reined up just inside the gate hole.

"You hadn't ought to do that . . . here."

Dexter saw the startled look on Cliff's face and the awful embarrassment of Rezin, and broke into laughter. Berl looked at the sheriff disgustedly.

"You got the darndest sense of humor," he said.

Center Point Publishing
600 Brooks Road ● PO Box 1
Thorndike ME 04986-0001 USA

(207) 568-3717

US & Canada:
1 800 929-9108
www.centerpointlargeprint.com